I0592688

THE IDENTITY THIEF
COLLECTION

STELLA BRUNO INVESTIGATES

PETER MULRANEY

Cover image: Jimmy Bay on Unsplash.

ISBN-13: 978-0-6482523-0-6

This edition published 2018.

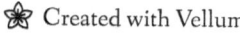 Created with Vellum

CONTENTS

THE IDENTITY THIEF

STELLA BRUNO INVESTIGATES

Stella observed the blue plastic tent and its ring of crime scene tape as Brian parked alongside the patrol car in the rear car park of the Old Spot Hotel in Salisbury Heights. There were two other vehicles parked near the patrol car. One was marked as a police vehicle. The other she recognised as the Coroner's van.

Brian killed the engine. Stella stepped out of their air-conditioned cocoon into a north wind pushing dry air from the overheated interior of the continent towards the coast. It ruffled her short dark hair and stung her face. She walked around to Brian's side of the car, out of the wind, to slip into her scene-of-crime suit.

Stella thought it was hot enough for her to melt in her skirt and blouse without the extra layer of required protective clothing. She'd only been out of the car for a couple of minutes but it felt like she'd been standing in a sauna for hours by the time she'd donned the suit.

She watched as Brian struggled into his disposable suit, sitting on the driver's seat to pull on his blue plastic bag shoes, and wondered if he was about to keel over on her.

'You need to lose some weight, Brian.'

'Think I've lost three kilos since I got out of the car, Sarge.'

'Couple of beers will take care of that.'

'If I live long enough to get into the bar.'

Stella noted the lack of onlookers standing around. With the mercury pushing towards forty degrees Celsius, she assumed anybody with any sense would be inside, standing in the eighteen-degree air-conditioned interior of the hotel, and planned on joining them as soon as she could.

They walked over to the constable standing in the shade of the blue tent. Stella flashed her ID and they entered the crime scene.

The tent covered a new looking white Mitsubishi Lancer. While the tent provided shade and protection from the wind, it was suffocatingly hot under its flapping blue plastic. Stella looked into the car. The body of a grey-haired man with matching beard occupied the driver's seat of the Lancer, held in place by the seat belt. The inside of the windscreen was splattered with blood and brains, thanks to the bullet that had entered his head from behind his right ear and exited above his left eye.

'How long's he been here, Steve?' Stella asked the pathologist with the crime scene investigators.

Steve Wright looked up from his task. 'Hello, Stella. Nice to see you, too.'

'Steve, it's too bloody hot to stand around making small talk.'

Steve smiled. 'I'd say we were lucky someone spotted him this morning. He'd be a right old stinker if he'd spent a few days like today locked in here.'

'So, you reckon he was killed last night, then?'

'Probably.'

'Any sign of the round?'

'Nine mill. Got it bagged.'

Stella glanced at the body. 'Any ID on him?'

'Driver's licence and a couple of credit cards.'

Stella waited while Brian snapped a copy of the driver's

licence and credit cards with his iPhone and wondered why the killer hadn't bothered taking the victim's ID.

'I've got people to talk to, Steve. Send me your report.' She didn't wait for him to respond. She knew he'd be thorough.

Once they were back by the car, Stella stripped off her scene-of-crime suit and waited for Brian to do the same. When Brian had stowed their discarded suits in the boot of the car, they headed towards the constable standing at the back door of the hotel.

Stella showed him her ID. 'Who's inside?'

'Sergeant Murray. He's got the bloke who found the body and the hotel manager in the back bar, Sergeant.'

'Thanks.'

Stella could feel her perspiration freezing across her shoulders as soon as she walked into the back bar where three men sat at a table talking. The man in the uniform stood as Stella and Brian approached them.

Stella thought he looked too young to be a sergeant. She held up her ID. 'DS Bruno. This is DC Rhodes.'

'Simon Murray.'

Stella shook his hand. 'Who found the body?'

Simon introduced Matt Brewer, the day manager of the drive-through bottle shop.

'Spotted him when I came in. Thought he was asleep.' Matt looked at the older man sitting at the table. 'Didn't think anybody in his right mind would want to sit out there in this heat, so I went to see if he was okay. That's when I saw the mess on the windscreen and realised he was dead.'

'Did you touch anything?' said Stella.

'No. I didn't even need to open the door to see he'd been shot.'

Stella wondered if Matt had been working the previous night. 'When do you knock off?'

'Around six. Andrew does the night shift.'

'Who are you?' said Stella, turning her attention to the other man at the table.

'Michael James. I manage the hotel.'

'We'll need to talk to whoever was working last night.'

'I've given their details to Sergeant Murray.'

'I've got people out taking statements,' said Sergeant Murray.

Stella nodded to let him know she'd heard him. She liked it when Uniform used their initiative and updated her appraisal of Simon Murray. He seemed to know what was expected of him.

'Did either of you know the victim?'

'He's been coming in for a meal every Thursday night for the last few years. Usually eats in here and then spends a couple of hours on the pokies,' said Michael. 'Said his name was Bob, but I don't really know anything else about him.'

'I've never seen him before,' said Matt.

Stella turned to Brian. 'What's the name on the driver's licence?'

'Robert Cunningham.'

'Doesn't ring any bells,' said Michael.

'Did he meet people here that you noticed?'

'No-one that I noticed. We get a lot of single older people in here for a meal and a play on the pokies. They seem more interested in the pokies than each other.'

Stella didn't want to imagine what that sort of life would be like.

'Do you have CCTV?'

'In the gaming areas and at the entrances but nothing outside in the back car park.'

'Can we take a look at last night's recording?'

Michael escorted them to his office and switched on the bank of monitors on the wall.

'He usually played in the small room. That monitor there.'

He pointed to the screen in the top right-hand corner. 'Just let me find last night's file.'

'What time did he generally come in?' said Stella.

'He was pretty regular. Arrived around seven and was usually gone by ten. Here it is.'

They watched the victim walk into the small gaming room and sit at one of the machines at nineteen forty-eight, according to the time stamp, and play until twenty-one fifteen when his mobile phone rang. He left the room immediately after taking the call at twenty-one eighteen.

'We have a camera over the back entrance,' said Michael. 'It will come up on the screen under that one.' They waited while he located the file and then watched the victim leave the hotel by the door that led out into the rear car park at twenty-one twenty-three.

'That's a five minute gap,' said Stella.

'Probably went for a piss on the way out,' said Brian.

'Would you have last Thursday's file by any chance?' said Stella.

They watched the victim do a repeat performance and leave after receiving a phone call at twenty-one thirty-six.

According to his driver's licence, Robert Cunningham lived in the Vineyard Retirement Village in South Gawler, a twenty-minute drive up Main North Road from the Old Spot Hotel.

Brian parked the car in front of the Community Centre, located alongside a bowling green, in the middle of the gated community of one hundred and forty residential units that made up the retirement village.

Stella surveyed the streets of landscaped gardens and neat lawns.

'This is May's idea of retirement,' said Brian.

'You sure you want to move into a retirement village?'

'She's already looking. There's a waiting list for most of them, unless you go to Mt Gambier.'

'Mt Gambier?'

'Yeah. They're advertising vacancies.'

'Seriously, Brian, Mt Gambier?'

'Her sisters live there.'

'But aren't all your friends here?'

'I don't think she's thinking about my friends.'

'How long before you retire?'

'Another five years, I hope.'

'Mt Gambier.' Stella shook her head as she opened the car door. 'You need to work on her, Brian. You'll die of boredom down there.'

They entered the Community Centre and approached the woman sitting behind the counter at reception.

'Can I help you?'

Stella held up her ID. 'Police. We'd like to speak to the manager.'

'Just a moment, I'll see if Mrs Hill is available.'

The place appeared deserted and Stella guessed everyone was sitting inside with their air-conditioners on. She knew that's what she'd be doing if she wasn't working.

'How long's this heat wave supposed to last?'

'Supposed to be a big thunder storm later tonight. Think I heard them say it would be thirty something with high humidity tomorrow.'

'As if that's any better than this.'

'At least this place is air-conditioned,' said Brian.

'Mrs Hill can see you now,' said the receptionist, who directed them to an office two doors down the corridor behind her.

'How can I help you, Sergeant?'

'I'm investigating a murder at the Old Spot Hotel.'

'Oh, yes, saw something about that on the morning news. What does that have to do with us?'

'Appears the victim lived here,' said Stella. 'We'd like access to his unit.'

'Who are we talking about?' said Mrs Hill.

'Robert Cunningham. According to his driver's licence he lived in unit 65.'

'Bob,' said Mrs Hill. 'Are you sure it's him?'

'Show her the driver's licence, Brian.'

Mrs Hill examined the image on Brian's iPhone. 'That's him, alright.' She looked at Stella. 'This is dreadful.'

'Murder is never pleasant, I'm afraid,' said Stella. 'Do you have any next of kin details, Mrs Hill? We'll need to notify them.'

Mrs Hill sat down behind her desk. 'Let me check.'

They waited while she searched through the files on her computer.

'I'm afraid not, Sergeant. From what's on file it looks like he never married and he hasn't listed any next of kin.'

Stella looked at Brian, who was writing in his notebook.

'When did he move in?'

'He's been with us for just under five years. Model resident as far as I'm aware. Never late with his service payments, no complaints from his neighbours.'

'Is that unusual?' said Stella.

Mrs Hill smiled. 'Not everyone ages gracefully, Sergeant.'

'Does your file have his previous address listed? We may need to talk to his neighbours.'

'He told us he lived at 28 Gladstone Terrace, Prospect, before moving here.'

Stella waited while Brian wrote that down. 'Can you let us into his unit?'

'You don't have his key?'

'His personal belongings from the scene are still with Forensics. I assumed you'd have a master key.'

'Let me call security. They have the master keys in case of emergencies.'

—————

Stella pulled on a pair of latex gloves as she stepped into the living room of unit 65.

'Turn on the bloody air conditioner, Brian. We'll die in here.'

Brian spotted the remote on the kitchen bench and activated the air conditioner. The apartment was compact, so it didn't take long for the split unit mounted on the back wall of the kitchen to fill the space with cold air.

There was a bedroom and a study off the living area, a separate kitchen and a combined bathroom and laundry. Stella peered out of the kitchen window into the small paved courtyard. Brian opened the door in the wall of the living room and inspected the empty single car garage.

'You check the bedroom. I'll have a look at what's in the study,' said Stella, when Brian returned from the garage.

Stella opened the drawers of the desk under the small window that looked out onto the street. The top drawer held an assortment of pens and paper clips. The bottom drawer, more like a small filing cabinet, held a collection of personal papers, including several copies of Robert Cunningham's birth certificate, a copy of the contract of sale for 28 Gladstone Terrace, a signed copy of his agreement with Vineyard Retirement Village, and the details of his Commonwealth Superannuation payments.

Stella boxed up the contents of the bottom drawer. The only other item of interest in the study was a laptop computer. Stella added it to the box, along with its associated cord and charger.

'Find anything, Brian?'

'Only this, Sarge.' Brian walked into the study with a small wooden box in his hands. 'Our boy had a loaded 9mm Luger on the top shelf of his wardrobe.'

'I didn't see a gun licence in his papers,' said Stella.

'Maybe it's in his wallet,' said Brian, 'but these things are supposed to be stored in a locked cabinet.'

'Make it safe and put it in the box.'

While Brian secured the box of items they had taken from the apartment in the boot of the car, Stella rang the doorbell of unit 64 and waited in the shade at the front of the building. Brian had rejoined her by the time the door was opened by an elderly woman.

'Hello.'

'Hi, I'm Detective Sergeant Bruno.' Stella held out her ID. 'I'd like to ask you a few questions about your neighbour.'

'Well, you'd better come in, then.' She opened the screen door and let them in.

Stella noted that the apartment was the mirror image of number 65.

'Would you like a cold drink?'

'That would be wonderful,' said Stella.

'Thank you,' said Brian.

Their hostess opened her fridge and a few moments later they were sitting around her table sipping glasses of ice-cold water.

'How long have you lived here, in the village?' said Stella.

'We moved in when Clem retired. That was twenty years ago. We lived in a double unit then. Number 24. I moved in here after Clem died. That would be ten years ago next month.'

'Can you tell me your name, please?'

'Doris Appleby, but, please, call me Doris.'

'Thank you, Doris.' Stella took another sip of her water.

'Who do you want to know about, love?'

'The man that lives in number 65. Robert Cunningham.'

'Bob? Everyone calls him Bob. He's usually home on Fridays but I haven't seen him today.'

'I'm afraid I have some bad news about that, Doris. The reason we're here is we're investigating his murder.'

Stella thought Doris was going to spill her glass of water and reached across the table and steadied her shaking hands. 'I'm sorry. That's probably come as a bit of a shock.'

Doris took a couple of deep breaths and shook her head. 'Who would want to kill Bob? He was such a nice man. A real gentleman.'

'What can you tell us about him?'

'I was surprised he'd never married. If I were twenty years younger, I would have chased him myself.' She smiled at Stella. 'It gets lonely being on your own. I've got everything I want and the young ones come to see me, but it's not the same now that Clem's gone.'

Stella nodded her agreement. She knew what it was like to be the one left behind after a visit from the grim reaper.

'Do you know who he mixed with in the village?'

'He was very friendly. He was always talking to someone. But you should probably talk to Sheila McGregor in number 44. He spent a lot of time with her. I thought they'd get together after her Henry died.'

'Did he tell you anything about himself?'

'Told me he'd been a public servant, but he always joked that he'd have to kill me if he told me anything about what he'd actually done.'

Stella looked at Brian, who shrugged his shoulders and made a note.

'What about visitors? Did Bob have many visitors?'

Doris looked at her hands. 'You know, now that you mention

it, I don't think he did. He went out a bit but I don't recall seeing anyone come to visit. Not anyone from outside the village, in any case. I usually have the blinds up and the door open when it's not hot like this.' She looked up. 'When I'm just sitting here reading I can see the front of his place.'

They walked over to number 44 and rang the doorbell.

'Be with you in a minute!'

They waited in the shade on the porch.

The door opened. 'Oh, hello. Can I help you?'

'Mrs McGregor?'

'Yes.'

'Detective Sergeant Bruno.' Stella held up her ID. 'Mind if we come in?'

Stella guessed Sheila McGregor was in her late sixties. She certainly moved with a lot more energy than the elderly Doris Appleby as she ushered them into her apartment.

'What brings you here?' said Sheila, as they stood inside her living room enjoying the cool air blowing across them from the air conditioner mounted above her kitchen window.

'Robert Cunningham.'

'Bob. What's he been up to? I didn't think he was the type to get in trouble with the police.'

Stella smiled. 'I understand you're close friends. Is that right?'

Stella noticed a blush rise and fade in Sheila's neck.

'I suppose you could say that. He's been good to me since my husband died.'

'I think you'd better sit down, Mrs McGregor, I'm afraid I have some bad news.'

'What sort of bad news?' said Sheila, sinking into the couch and looking from Stella to Brian.

'I'm sorry, but Bob's dead. He's been murdered.'

Sheila sank back into the couch. 'Murdered? When did this happen?'

Stella sat down beside her on the couch.

'We're not sure yet but probably sometime last night.'

'Where?'

'At the Old Spot Hotel.'

Sheila reached for a tissue and blew her nose. 'What was he doing there?'

'Apparently, he went there for a meal every Thursday night.'

'Oh, I knew he went to the city every Thursday, but I had no idea he was stopping off there on the way home.'

'Do you know why he went to the city on Thursdays?'

'Told me he met up with some of his mates from work but I've never met any of them.'

'Do you know where he used to work?'

'He only ever said he'd worked for the government.' She chuckled. 'He always said he'd have to kill us if he told us anything about what he'd done for them. He was such a wag.'

'I take it you didn't know him before he moved into the village?'

Sheila shook her head. 'We moved in around the same time. Bob hit it off with my husband before he died. They spent a lot of time playing lawn bowls and flirting with the older ladies. But that all came to an end when Henry had his heart attack. Bob seemed to lose interest in the bowls after that.'

'Do you know if he had any enemies?'

'Not that he mentioned.'

'What about here in the village? Anyone he'd upset?'

Sheila looked down at the floor. 'I suppose he might have upset James over in 46. He fancies me but Bob was a lot more fun. I hardly think James would have been jealous enough to kill him though. Besides, he's a retired minister.'

'Do you know if Bob had any next of kin we need to talk to?'

'He didn't have any family. Said he'd never married.' She paused and looked up to the right. 'Told me his parents were dead, and that his brother died when they were still young. Some kind of boating accident.'

Stella stood. She was ready to leave.

'We'll need someone to identify the body. Would you be prepared to do that?'

Sheila nodded. 'At least I've had some practice at that. We ran the funeral home in Clare before we retired.'

'I'll let you know when you need to come in.'

They rang the bell at number 46 but James Murphy wasn't home.

CHAPTER 2

WHEN THEY ARRIVED BACK at the office, DI Williams, who was overseeing the investigation as part of his caseload, was waiting to speak to Stella, who had operational responsibility for solving the crime.

The inspector was sitting at his desk looking at his computer screen when Stella walked into his office. He looked up from the screen but didn't invite her to sit. 'What have we got, Bruno?'

Stella felt her bristles rising. She hated the way he talked to her as if she was still a junior constable and not an experienced detective sergeant and suspected it was because she was the only woman on his team.

Frank Williams had been an arsehole when she'd first met him as a detective sergeant, not long after she had become a detective constable. That experience had taught her to be wary of the man and his habit of claiming credit and allocating blame. The promotion to detective inspector hadn't improved his character in Stella's estimation, even if he had shown himself to be an astute investigator, so she was always on her guard in his presence.

'A retired public servant with a bullet through his head, no witnesses, no apparent motive, and a lot of questions.'

'Go on.'

'I've spoken to the people at the retirement village where he lived. They don't know shit about him.' She shook her head. 'Sounds like he spun them some yarn about what he'd done for a living. Anyway, as far they're concerned, he was mister nice guy. We picked up a pile of documents from his apartment that should help with background checks, and he had a loaded pistol in his bedroom.'

'A pistol?'

'A 9mm Luger, to be precise.'

'That could be interesting. Does he have a gun licence?'

'That's something we're looking into.'

'Any next of kin?'

'Nothing on record at the retirement village.'

'Anything else?'

'We watched the CCTV from the hotel. Someone called the victim on his mobile just before he left the gaming room.'

'Gaming room?'

'According to the manager, he dropped in every Thursday night for a meal and spent a couple of hours playing the pokies.'

'Anyone who can identify the body?'

'I've got a Sheila McGregor, one of his neighbours from the retirement village but I'd like to find someone who knew him before he moved to the village five years ago. I've got a previous address in Prospect. Hopefully, we can find out where he worked from Commonwealth Superannuation.'

'Okay. Let me know if anything turns up in the background checks.'

When DI Williams turned back to his computer screen, Stella knew she'd been dismissed.

She returned to the squad room and drew up a list of the things she'd have to do the following day and then headed home.

It was deemed too hot for school sport on the Friday evening news, despite the impending overnight thunderstorm, so Stella enjoyed an extra Saturday morning hour in bed seeing she didn't have to make sure her son was ready to leave by seven am.

She wondered how people slept without air conditioning and then remembered what it had been like growing up in the house next door before her parents had installed air conditioning. She chuckled to herself as she remembered her father complaining about the cost, and the pleas of her mother for relief from the heat in 'dis bloody country you bringa me to!'

Stella's long-suffering mother had come from the alpine region of the Veneto in Italy where it got freezing cold but nowhere near as hot as it did in Adelaide during the summer. Stella was still amazed that her mother had stayed. It must have been a challenge coming half way around the world to live in a country where she didn't know anyone, apart from her new husband, and didn't speak the language. Stella was glad she did.

She got dressed and made her way into the kitchen for a quick breakfast before heading in to the office. Police work didn't stop because it was Saturday, especially work on a new investigation. DI Williams might be having the weekend off but she and Brian had work to do. She popped an English muffin into the toaster and the coffee percolator onto the stove.

'What are you doing today, Josh?' Stella asked, as her son appeared at the breakfast table in boxer shorts and a T-shirt.

'Homework.'

'Surely that won't take all day.'

'Nonna's taking us to the pictures after lunch.'

'Oh, what are you going to see?'

'The Boss Baby.'

'That looks like fun.'

'Yeah, she reckons it will help us understand Nonno.' Josh laughed. 'She's always stirring him up.'

'She's been like that for a long time, mate.'

'Don't know how Nonno puts up with it.'

'Guess that's why they call it love.'

Josh filled his bowl with Weet-Bix. 'Were you like that with Dad?'

Stella stopped eating and looked across the room at Rick's photo on the wall of the family room. 'No, your father was nothing like your grandfather. He had a sense of humour to start with.'

'I wish he was still here.'

'Me, too.'

Josh poured cold milk over his cereal. 'What are you doing today?'

'I've got a new case, a murder.'

'Is that the one at the Old Spot Hotel?'

'Yeah. Bit of a mystery though.'

'What do you mean?'

'No motive. The victim was a retired public servant. Everybody is saying he was a nice guy.'

'Maybe they shot the wrong guy.'

'Think you've been watching too much TV with Nonno. Criminals do some stupid things, mate, but they usually shoot the right person.'

Stella looked at her watch. 'I gotta go. I'll see you tonight and you can tell me all about Boss Baby.' She kissed him on the cheek and tousled his hair 'Love you.'

'Love you, Mum.'

Brian was at his desk in the squad room when Stella arrived.

'Couldn't you sleep, Brian?'

'Too many loose ends. Couldn't stop thinking about our man, Bob. Besides, May wanted me out of the house. We got people coming over for dinner tonight and she reckons I mess things up as soon as she's cleaned.'

Stella made herself a coffee and pulled her chair up next to Brian's desk. She thought Brian and May were as bad as her parents when it came to being together in the same place. 'What's bothering you about the victim?'

'Cunningham doesn't have a licence for that Luger. I checked before I went home last night. Wish I'd waited until this morning.'

'Yeah, I've been wondering about our man as well. Why would anyone want to shoot a retired public servant that's such a nice guy? Is he on any of our databases?'

Brian leant back in his chair. 'The only database he's on is motor vehicles. I checked his driver's licence and the registration of the Lancer. Everything looks in order. He doesn't even have a speeding ticket. Too clean for me.'

Stella wondered whether their victim had reinvented himself when he moved into the retirement village or if he'd always been a nice guy. 'I think we should door knock his neighbours in Prospect. Someone might remember him. It's only five years since he sold the house and moved into the retirement village.'

'That might be a good idea, Sarge.'

'Get a request into Telstra for his mobile phone records. Be interesting to find out who called him on Thursday night.'

'What about asking Com Super if they can shed any light on his employment? They should be able to tell us what agency he worked for.'

'We'll have to leave that until Monday. They're closed on weekends.' Stella moved over to her own desk and logged on. 'Let me see if anything's come through from Forensics or Uniform.'

When her PC booted up, Stella read an email from Sergeant Murray, which listed the details of the hotel employees working on Thursday night, and advised her that none of them had seen anything.

Next, she read the interim report from Forensics, which confirmed what she already knew: Robert Cunningham had been shot in the head at close range with a 9mm pistol. The only new bit of information was a note from the ballistics analyst informing her that the same weapon had been used in an unsolved gangland killing two years ago in Victoria.

'What do you make of this, Brian?' She showed him the note from the ballistics analyst.

'Suggests he was assassinated by someone in the underworld. I wonder what our man got himself mixed up in after retiring from the public service?'

'Or before,' said Stella.

'Do you think they might have bumped off the wrong man? Wouldn't be the first case of mistaken identity.'

'That's what Josh said.'

'How is he?'

'Pretty good for a fourteen-year-old being spoilt rotten by his grandparents.'

'You're lucky to have them.'

'Tell me about it. I wouldn't be here doing this if it weren't for them. Come on, let's go and speak to the people in Gladstone Terrace.'

Although the overnight thunderstorm had dumped five millimetres of rain on the city, at ten in the morning, when Stella rang the doorbell of number 26 Gladstone Terrace, the air temperature was already above thirty degrees with a humidity reading close to one hundred percent. Stella could feel her dress sticking to her body as she admired the neat front lawn edged with rose bushes.

Brian had sensibly left his suit coat in the car but perspiration was dripping from his face.

The front door edged open behind a locked security door that blocked Stella's view of whoever had opened the door.

'We don't do Jehovah's Witnesses,' said a male voice.

'Police,' said Stella, holding up her ID.

'What the fuck do you want?'

'I'd like to ask you a few questions. Would you mind opening the door so I can see you? I don't like talking to shadows.'

'I don't like talking to the police.'

'It's not about you. I want to know about the man that lived in number 28 until five years ago. Can you help me?'

There was click, and the door opened. A middle-aged man with a well-developed beer gut, a silver goatee, and tattoos on his arms stepped out onto the porch. He towered over Stella in his shorts and navy blue singlet but was matched in height and weight by Brian.

'I'm Detective Sergeant Bruno. This is Detective Constable Rhodes. Do you mind telling us your name?'

'John Schmidt.'

'Have you lived here long, Mr Schmidt?'

'Around twenty years.'

Mr Schmidt, we're investigating the murder of Robert Cunningham, who I understand lived next door. Did you know him?'

'Yeah.'

'Have much to do with him?'

'A bit. He wasn't that social. Kept to himself a lot.'

'Do you think you'd recognise him?'

'Probably.'

Brian showed him the image of the victim's driver's licence.

'Looks a bit like him, but I couldn't say for sure. Do you have anything clearer?'

'Not yet, I'm afraid.'

'Hang on a minute. I think I have a photo of him on my phone. We had lunch at the Bombay Bicycle Club when he retired. My phone was new then. Took pictures everywhere we went.'

John went inside and came back with an iPhone in his hand. He scrolled through his images. 'Here it is.' He held it out for Stella to look at.

'You sure that's him?' said Stella.

'That's my wife sitting next to him.'

'Can you send me a copy of that?'

'Sure. What's your email address?'

Stella handed him her card. 'It's on there.' She waited while John keyed in her email address and sent her the image.

'Were you surprised he sold up and moved into a retirement village?'

'Not really. He was pretty sick there for a while after he retired. Came home from hospital one week and sold up the next. Didn't even come over and say goodbye.'

'That strike you as strange?'

'Well, as I said, he wasn't all that social.'

'Do you know where he worked?'

'For the ABS, you know, the Bureau of Stats. He was some kind of mathematician. Maybe that's why he was so weird. My wife liked him though.'

'Is she home?'

John looked past Stella to the rose bushes. 'She's no longer with us. I scattered her ashes around the rose bushes. She loved those bloody roses.'

'Oh, I'm sorry to hear that.'

'It's okay. She's not suffering now.'

Stella thanked Mr Schmidt for his help and they walked up the street to number 30.

The couple in number 30 had only moved in a few months ago but the woman in number 27 across the street had lived in the house all her life.

'He was a weird one, love. I reckon he was one of those homosexuals. Only ever saw other men visiting him. Never a woman.'

'Is this him?'

Brian showed her the image from the victim's licence.

'Looks like him but he's put on some weight if that's him. He was frightfully skinny when he came out of the hospital.'

'Which hospital, do you know?'

'He was in the RAH. The Royal Adelaide. We all thought he was going to die, and then he sold up and disappeared.'

'Do you know why he had been in the hospital?'

'Poor man had chronic leukaemia. He'd had it for years.'

CHAPTER 3

AFTER MONDAY MORNING'S autopsy of the victim tentatively identified as Robert Cunningham, Stella suspected she had a problem. There was no sign the body in the morgue had belonged to someone who had suffered from leukaemia in any of its forms. She relayed her suspicion to DI Williams.

'We'll need to access his medical records to confirm my information, sir.'

'Do that. Have you spoken to anyone at the Bureau of Stats?'

'I have an appointment at two o'clock with a Myles Christopher.'

'Let me know what transpires. This is starting to look messy, Bruno.'

Stella returned to the squad room. 'Any luck with motor vehicles, Brian?'

'They reckon this licence is a fake. A very good one, mind you, but not one of theirs and the image they have on file matches the image Mr Schmidt gave us. Our man resembles Cunningham but I doubt he's the genuine article.'

'He hasn't had leukaemia either. Come on, we need to go to the RAH so we can verify the information we got on Saturday.'

'We'll need a warrant for that, won't we?'

'Got one.'

'Have you uploaded the images from Forensics?'

'I've got the cleaned up one.'

They had to wait at the RAH but they left with a copy of the medical record of the Robert Cunningham who had lived at 28 Gladstone Terrace, Prospect, and his vital statistics did not match those of the body in the police morgue as far as Stella could tell.

On their way back to the office, they stopped in at the Australian Bureau of Statistics in Waymouth Street to meet with Myles Christopher.

'We're trying to confirm the identity of a man killed on Thursday night.'

'Is this the man found in the car park at the Old Spot?'

'Yes. He had this driver's licence on him, which we now know is counterfeit,' said Stella.

Myles studied the images on the screen of Brian's iPhone. 'Well, I admit he looks a bit like Bob but that's not the man that worked here.'

'You sure about that?'

'I worked with him for ten years, Sergeant. That's not him.'

'Have you heard from him since he retired?'

'The last time I saw him he was in the RAH. To be honest, I'm surprised I haven't read his funeral notice in the paper but, now that you mention it, I don't think I have heard from him since then.'

'That strike you as strange?'

'A lot of people that work here are what you'd call introverts. You know, the type that keep to themselves. They tend to drop off the radar when they leave work, so I guess it's not all that unusual.'

'Would you be prepared to sign a sworn statement about what you've just told us?'

'Certainly, Sergeant. I don't know who your man is, but he

certainly isn't Bob Cunningham.'

As soon as they returned to the office in Angas Street, Stella double checked the autopsy report against the medical record she had collected from the hospital. The victim didn't even have the same blood group as the Robert Cunningham who had been admitted to the RAH.

She picked up her desk telephone and called DI Williams.

'I don't know who we have in the morgue, sir, but it's not the Robert Cunningham that worked for the ABS or lived at 28 Gladstone Terrace.'

'That gives you a few puzzles to solve then, Bruno.'

***

Stella sat at her desk looking through the documents they had collected from the victim's apartment and listening to Brian questioning someone in the Office of the Registrar of Births, Deaths and Marriages about Robert Cunningham.

Brian clunked the receiver back into its cradle on his desk. 'Well, officially, Cunningham is still alive, Sarge. At least, they don't have a record of his death.'

'Looks like he hasn't changed his address with his bank or Com Super either. Everything's been going to Post Office Box 125, Prospect.'

'But, if they're in that pile, that means our man was collecting his mail.'

'Might explain why he came to the city every Thursday. Have a look through the personal effects Forensics bagged at the crime scene and see if he had a key to a post office box.'

Brian retrieved the plastic bag of personal effects from the evidence locker and looked through the keys on the victim's keyring. 'This looks like one.'

'Well, let's go and see if it works.'

It took them fifteen minutes to negotiate traffic and park outside the Post Office on Prospect Road. Brian inserted the key into box 125 and opened the door. The box was empty. They went inside.

Stella showed her ID to the woman at the counter. 'Detective Sergeant Bruno. I'd like some information on the holder of one of your post office boxes. The one that goes with this key.'

'What number is it?'

'One hundred and twenty-five.'

The woman consulted a list on her computer. 'That's assigned to a Mr Robert Cunningham.'

'What residential address do you have for him?'

'Looks like his residential address is a unit in a retirement village in Gawler South.'

'Do you know when he accessed his box to pick up his mail?'

'Just a minute.'

The woman disappeared into the room behind the counter, from where Stella could hear her talking with someone but not what they were saying. A couple of minutes later she came back out to the counter.

'According to Phil, who sorts the mail, Mr Cunningham didn't get much mail, but it seemed to disappear on a Thursday afternoon when he did.'

'You might want to hold any mail that comes for him from now on. The man that had this key is dead, and if anyone turns up claiming to be Robert Cunningham, please call me on this number.' Stella handed her one of her cards.

They stood outside and surveyed the cars in the car park. It was still hot but at least the air temperature was down to what Stella considered a more bearable thirty-two.

'Not looking good for Cunningham, Sarge, if this other bloke was collecting his mail.'

'I was thinking the same thing, Brian. Let's go see if anyone is home at 28 Gladstone Terrace.'

It took them less than five minutes to drive around to 28 Gladstone Terrace. The door was opened by a young woman holding a small boy on her hip.

'Can I help you?'

Stella held up her ID. 'Hi. I'm Detective Sergeant Bruno and this is Detective Constable Rhodes. Do you mind telling us how long you've lived here?'

'Bit over five years. Why?'

'In that case, I'd like to ask you a few questions about what you found in the house when you moved in.'

The young woman shrugged her shoulders. 'Do you want to come in?'

She led them through the house to the family room at the rear.

'Is this bit new?' said Stella.

'Yes, we had this built just before Jamie was born.'

'What was here before you added this room?'

The woman pointed to the kitchen bench. 'That's where the back wall used to be. This part was like a lean-to laundry. We have a new laundry through there.' She pointed to a door in the opposite wall.

'I like what you've done,' said Stella.

'My sister's an architect. She designed it for us.' She smiled. 'What is it you want to know about the house?' She placed her son on the floor among his toys.

'Did you meet the man you purchased the house from?' said Stella.

'Mr Cunningham? No, we only dealt with the agent.'

'Was there anything about the house that looked new or out of place when you moved in?' said Stella.

'Like what?'

'New flooring, built-in robes, things like that. Maybe a new feature in the garden.'

'There was nothing new or updated in the house which is probably why we got it for such a good price, but there was a new concrete floor in the garden shed.'

'Where's that?' said Stella.

The young woman opened the curtains and pointed into the backyard. 'Over there.'

Stella looked at the shed in the far corner of the backyard. It had seen better days, in her opinion, but with a glory vine growing on a trellis attached to the side facing the house it had that characteristic old-world garden shed appearance she'd seen in House & Garden.

'Can you show us inside the shed?'

'Why?'

'Just want to see how large the floor space is,' said Stella.

'Three metres by two. We thought if we added a window it might make a nice cubby house for Jamie when he's older.'

Stella looked at Brian.

'Be big enough.'

'What's going on?' said the young householder.

'We might have to dig up the floor of that shed,' said Stella.

'What?'

'We're trying to find Mr Cunningham.'

The woman's hand went to her mouth. 'And you think he could be buried under the shed?'

'I don't know for sure but someone's been impersonating him for the last five years.'

'Why don't you ask him?'

'I wish I could,' said Stella, 'but I can't. He's in the morgue.'

The young woman looked from Stella to Brian. 'So what happens now?'

'We'll get a search warrant and you'll get a new floor in your shed. Perhaps a new shed.'

It was late Tuesday afternoon when Forensics arrived at 28 Gladstone Terrace in an unmarked van and backed up the driveway. The team entered the backyard through the carport and dismantled the garden shed before erecting one of their blue tents over the corner of the yard where the shed had stood.

Stella sat in the family room chatting with John and Anne Summers about everything happening in the world, except what was going on in their backyard.

By nightfall, the concrete slab had been cut up and removed, piece by piece, to reveal a depression in the soil beneath. The team ran a cord from a socket in the carport to power their lights and the tent took on a spooky glow. Two hours later, Brian came into the house and called Stella out to the tent.

When she entered the tent the team was standing around what looked like a freshly dug grave, drinking coffee from styrofoam cups. The sergeant in charge shone a torch into the hole and asked Stella to take a look at what they had unearthed.

The torch illuminated a skull embedded in the soil at the bottom of the trench.

Stella called DI Williams to let him know what they had found.

'Let me know when you have a positive ID, Bruno. And, Sergeant. Good work.'

Stella nearly dropped her phone. 'Thank you, sir.'

It was several more hours before the skeleton had been extracted and packed for its journey to the forensic pathology laboratory.

By the time Stella arrived in the office on Wednesday, Forensics had used Robert Cunningham's dental records to verify that they had, in fact, found his skeleton.

There was also a line in their report informing her they had recovered a 9mm bullet from inside the skull which suggested to Stella that Cunningham had not died from leukaemia or any other natural cause.

As she was preparing to leave for the day, Stella heard the ping of an email notification. She opened the email and read the attached report from Forensics' ballistics analyst, in which he advised that the bullet found inside Cunningham's skull had been fired from the Luger she and Brian had retrieved from the apartment the Old Spot's victim had occupied at the Vineyard Retirement Village.

She called DI Williams and passed on the information.

'Still doesn't solve your original problem, Bruno. Who's that fellow in the morgue, and why is he there?'

'This Cunningham guy must have been a real loner if no-one noticed he was missing,' said Brian, as they waited in line to buy coffee.

'What do you mean?' said Stella.

'Think about it. He's been at the bottom of the garden for five years. Surely someone would have missed him?'

'Maybe he really doesn't have any next of kin.'

'No friends either, by the look of it.'

'That could be you, Brian, if May drags you off to Mt Gambier.'

They sat at a table with a view of the street.

'She's changed her mind about Mt Gambier. Too bloody cold in the winter, apparently. I could have told her that but she's not listening to me.' He shook his head. 'Now she wants to look at places down at Victor.'

'That's closer to the city, at least.'

'Yeah, and they've got some nice golf courses down there.'

"I didn't know you played golf, Brian.'

'Well, I haven't for years but I played a lot when I was younger.' He gave Stella a sheepish grin. 'And fitter.'

'I worry about you, Brian. You've been putting on a bit lately.'

Brian shifted in his seat and looked out past Stella to the traffic in the street. 'Doctor says I have to cut down on the sugar and get off my arse more, or I could end up with type two diabetes.'

'Shit, Brian! That sounds serious. What are you doing about it?'

'She's put me on a diet. No booze, and I have to eat like a rabbit and stay away from all my favourite foods.'

Stella sipped her latte. 'What about exercise? Isn't that supposed to help?'

'I'm going back to golf. I've renewed my membership at North Adelaide. Do you remember Jack Wynn?'

Stella nodded her head. She had fond memories of Jack Wynn. Jack had been Rick's sergeant at the time of the accident that had taken him from her. He'd taken Stella under his wing and helped her re-establish her career when she'd returned to work after Rick's death.

'He plays every morning. I'm going out with him two mornings a week.'

'Good for you. What's May think about that?'

'She's been at me about my weight for years. Now she's making me salad for lunch and begging me to get fit.'

'Guess she doesn't want to retire to Victor on her own, Brian.'

'Me neither.'

'What, retire to Victor or on your own?'

'On my own.'

Stella finished her latte and waited for Brian to finish his long black. 'What do you think we should do about our mystery man?'

'I was thinking we could ask Sheila McGregor if she had any

photographs of him. We need something better than what we have. Might be a bit of an ask for anyone to recognise him from any of those crime scene images.'

'Probably be a good idea to interview her again. She might see him a little differently now. You got her details on your phone?'

Brian nodded.

'Give her a call and see if she's available.'

Sheila McGregor opened the door as soon as they got out of the car and ushered them into her living room.

'Will I still need to identify the body?'

'I don't think that will be necessary now, Mrs McGregor. I think we have established that he was the man you knew as Bob Cunningham. Our challenge now is to find out who he was before he started pretending to be Bob,' said Stella.

'How do you think I can help you with that? I've told you all I know about him. I still can't understand how such a nice man could be a liar like that, though. I really liked Bob.'

'I guess it's all been a bit of a shock for you, Mrs McGregor. First finding out he'd been murdered and now finding out he wasn't who he said he was.'

'It's worse than one of those shows on TV. At least you know they're only make believe. This is just ridiculous. I feel like such a fool to have been taken in by him.'

'Don't be hard on yourself, Mrs McGregor. You weren't to know, and you certainly aren't alone. He fooled village management and the conveyancer he used to sell the real Mr Cunningham's house in Prospect. So he must have been a pretty good actor.'

'And good at counterfeiting documents,' said Brian.

'Remember that driver's licence we showed you? Looked real to me but it's a fake.'

Sheila smiled and invited them to sit down.

'Do you by any chance have any photographs of Bob?' said Stella. 'We need something other than the ones we took after he'd been shot.'

'Might have some of him on Facebook. Henry was always taking photos when we went places. Probably only group shots. I'm not sure I have any of Bob on his own. He wasn't keen on having his photograph taken. Guess we know why now.'

'Can you show us, please?' said Stella.

'Let me turn the computer on. I can't see anything on my phone these days. Come into the study.'

They waited while she fired up her laptop and logged on to Facebook.

'Here's one of him. I'd forgotten about this one.' She turned the laptop so they could see the screen.

'When was that taken?'

'About three months ago. We went on a bus trip up the river. It was organised by the village.'

'Do you think you could locate the original image,' said Brian.

'It would be on my phone.'

'Do you mind if I take a look?' said Brian.

'Let me get my phone.'

Sheila retrieved her mobile phone from the table in her living room. 'That's where the photos are, in there,' she said, handing her phone to Brian and pointing to the Photos icon.

Brian tapped on the icon and scrolled through the images until he spotted the one she had uploaded to Facebook. 'Looks like you took a few of Bob that day.'

'He was in a good mood. We'd stopped at a winery for lunch. He'd had a few before we got back on the bus.'

'Is it okay if I email these to myself?'

'If you think it will help.'

'Do you know if Bob was on Facebook?' said Stella.

'He didn't like Facebook but I'm pretty sure he was on that Twitter thing. He spent a lot of time on the internet. I think he had some sort of online business but he never went into the details with me. I remember him explaining it to Henry one time. Affiliate marketing or something like that I think it was called.' She looked at Stella and smiled. 'I don't even know what that is.'

'Me neither,' said Stella, 'but I'm sure Constable Rhodes knows what it is. He has a son that's into all that sort of thing.'

'Makes more money than I do,' said Brian. 'Perhaps I'll do some of that stuff when I retire, if my wife will let me.'

After speaking to Sheila McGregor, they walked over to unit 46 and rang the doorbell.

A white-haired man dressed in a shirt and tie opened the door. 'I suppose you want to talk about Bob. Sheila told me you were coming. Come in. Would you like a cup of tea?'

'That would be nice, thank you,' said Stella. 'By the way, I'm Detective Sergeant Bruno and this is Detective Constable Rhodes.'

'James Murphy. Come in.'

They sat in another tiny living room designed for one while James made the tea.

'The ladies seem to think Bob was wonderful, Mr Murphy. What was your impression of him?'

'Oh, he was a charmer alright.'

'What did he tell you he'd done before he retired?'

'Same story he told everybody else. I thought he must have been a spook. Either that or he liked to pull people's leg. He was always telling jokes.'

'Did he ever talk about his past?'

James poured the tea. Stella noticed he'd used a pot instead of offering individual tea bags. 'Funny you should ask that. Most people living here spend a great deal of time reminiscing about the past. I get to hear a fair bit of it being a retired minister. People seem to think I'm some sort of counsellor, and I suppose I am, but Bob only ever talked about the present day as if yesterday didn't exist.'

'You're aware that he wasn't actually Bob Cunningham?'

'Yes, Sheila did mention that. Came as a bit of a surprise, I can tell you. He might have been a bit of a wag but he was nice chap. Be interesting to find out who he really was.'

'Yes, it will be,' said Stella. 'Do you know if he had any visitors?'

'I suppose you know he went down to the city every Thursday?'

'Yes, we know that.'

James sipped his tea and then placed his cup back into its saucer. 'I didn't think much of it at the time, but a couple of Thursdays ago I noticed the District Nurse ringing his doorbell. I hadn't seen her before, and I'm pretty sure Bob hadn't been called on by the District Nurse before either. I asked her if she was looking for Bob and she said she was, so I told her he wasn't home and wouldn't be back until after dark.'

'Do you think you could describe her?'

'Not really. As you would imagine at this time of year, she was wearing sunglasses, but I'd say she was middle aged, I'd suppose. Maybe early forties. Hard to tell these days. About my height, a little overweight, and I think she had blonde hair.'

'Did she ever come back?'

'Not that I'm aware of.'

'Did you mention her visit to Bob?'

'Yes, the next day, but he said there must have been some mistake as he hadn't asked for a District Nurse to visit.'

CHAPTER 4

WHILE BRIAN CONCENTRATED on negotiating the south bound traffic on Main North Road, Stella placed a call to the Gawler office of the Royal District Nursing Service and asked about the abortive visit of a District Nurse to the Vineyard Retirement Village looking for Robert Cunningham.

'We don't have a Robert Cunningham listed as a client at that retirement village, Sergeant.'

Stella thought for a minute and wondered if someone had used the cover of being a District Nurse to confirm Bob, or whoever he was, lived there. 'Have any of your vehicles been stolen in the last month?'

'None of ours here at Gawler but the service has hundreds of vehicles. You'll need to check with head office.'

Stella thanked her for her cooperation and ended the call. She pulled the car's on-board computer towards her and spent several minutes interrogating the stolen vehicles database.

'Bloody hell! They've reported three cars stolen in the last month, and only two of them have been recovered.'

'What are you thinking, Sarge?'

'I'm thinking whoever killed Bob might have been playing at District Nurse to confirm his whereabouts.'

'How do you think they found him?'

'The same way we're hoping to. That photograph Mrs McGregor posted on Facebook.'

Brian glanced in her direction. 'She'll be mortified when she realises that he's been knocked off by a friend of a friend.'

Stella pushed the computer back towards the centre console. 'I wonder if she fully understands Facebook's privacy settings. She could be posting all of her stuff publicly without realising it.'

'I think Facebook gives you a reminder about that in your news feed.'

'You're right. I saw one the other night. But even if she changed her privacy settings it would be too late for anything she'd already posted publicly.'

Stella gazed out of the window and wondered how long it would be before there were no rural properties left between Adelaide and Gawler. Most of the suburban houses she could see as they drove back towards the city hadn't existed in her childhood, those far away days when her parents had started their annual trek to Barmera to spend the Australia Day long weekend with her father's brother and his family. She smiled as she recalled those long ago fun filled days sailing on Lake Bonney with her cousins. They all had kids of their own now, but her parents still made the annual trek, and she was grateful they took Josh with them so he'd get to know his country cousins.

Brian's voice brought her back into the present moment. 'I think we should send these photos to Victoria Police, Sarge. Maybe our man's someone they'd know, given the history of the gun used to kill him.'

'Worth a try, Brian.'

'Fancy hiding yourself away for five years only to have your cover blown by one of your new friends. What a bummer!'

'I guess you'd start letting your guard down if you'd pulled off an impersonation for five years, Brian.'

'I wonder who he was hiding from.'

Stella watched the rear of the car in front of them move closer as Brian slowed to stop at a red light. 'I wonder why he was hiding, and why he had to kill someone to do it.'

'Makes you think he must have been one of the bad guys.'

Stella scanned the log of calls received by the victim's mobile phone on the last Thursday night he had visited the Old Spot Hotel. There was only the one incoming call, the one they had watched him answer on the CCTV monitor in the hotel manager's office.

She checked the call log for the previous Thursday and saw the same number. Then she looked at Brian's handwritten note on the back of the page informing her he had established the number belonged to a public telephone in Grenfell Street in the city.

Stella turned her attention to the location data log, which listed the GPS coordinates of the victim's mobile phone as it broadcast its location to the towers in Telstra's mobile network. She noticed Brian had highlighted the data for the last two Thursdays, and added a note advising her that the lack of data indicated the victim had switched off his mobile phone in the morning as he'd left the retirement village and hadn't switch it back on until around seven pm, when he'd reached the Old Spot Hotel for his evening meal.

Stella looked at the photograph of the victim on the wall behind her desk. 'What were you doing on Thursdays, Bob, besides collecting the mail? And, who was calling you from Grenfell Street?'

She wondered why someone would only turn their mobile phone off on Thursdays and leave it on for every other day of the week. Her thinking was interrupted by Brian returning to his desk carrying the victim's laptop.

'What did you make of this?' She held up the papers he had left on her desk.

'I'd say our man knew a mobile phone could be used as a tracking device,' said Brian. 'Obviously, he didn't mind anyone knowing he was at the retirement village. After all, that was his cover, wasn't it?'

'But who'd get access to that data besides us? It's not like Telstra hands it out to anybody.'

'Good question, Sarge, but they do list the suburb you were in when you made a call on your account.'

'Maybe our man was up to something on Thursdays besides collecting the mail.'

'Not sure how we're going to find out what that was though, Sarge. It's not like we can ask him.'

'Perhaps someone will come forward now we have his photo out there. By the way, any luck with getting in to that laptop?'

'They cracked his password, so we're in. I'll let you know if I find anything.'

'I'll leave you to it. DI Williams wants to see me. Something's come up in the Genovese case.'

'Thought that was all ready to go to trial.'

'Me, too. But his nibs sounded like he's got his knickers in a twist.'

'Good luck.'

The Genovese trial was due to start the following Friday, so Stella wondered what DI Williams wanted to talk about. She thought they'd put together a watertight case, which was why the Director of Public Prosecutions had agreed to proceed.

She didn't recognise the other man in DI Williams' office when she entered but something about his energy field told her he was not a policeman.

'Ah, Sergeant Bruno. This is Shaun Porter from the DPP's office,' said DI Williams.

Must be someone new, she thought, as Shaun stood and extended his hand. Stella felt her breathing slow as he smiled at her, and a tingle ran up her arm when she shook his hand.

'Call me Shaun.'

'Stella.' She wasn't quite sure why she'd responded with her first name. After all, she was just establishing a professional relationship to assist the prosecution of the charges against another criminal, wasn't she?

'Take a seat, Sergeant.'

Stella was thankful DI Williams had asked her to sit. She wasn't quite sure what had just happened in that momentary exchange with Shaun Porter. She hadn't felt a response like that when meeting someone for quite some time. In fact, she'd decided after Rick's death it wasn't safe to access feelings like the ones she'd just felt.

'I'll let Shaun explain what's happened,' said DI Williams.

The dark look on the inspector's face told Stella he wasn't happy. She hoped she wasn't going to be blamed for whatever had pissed him off.

'Looks like we might have to drop the charges against Genovese. Our star witness has changed his mind,' said Shaun. 'He's refusing to testify. It's going to be a challenge getting a conviction without his testimony.'

'Does he understand his plea deal is off if he doesn't testify?' said Stella.

'I've explained that to him.'

'And?'

'Said he'd rather do the time than get a bullet in the head.'

'What's bought this on?' said DI Williams.

'I really don't know,' said Shaun.

'When did you find out he'd changed his mind?' said Stella.

'This morning.'

Stella thought about the timing. 'We have a body in the morgue, put there by a bullet fired from a handgun known to have been used in a gangland killing in Victoria,' said Stella.

'Is that the mystery man shot at the Old Spot Hotel?' said Shaun.

'Yes, and we went public with an appeal to identify him last night. I wonder if this is connected?' said Stella.

'Does Victoria Police have any idea who your man might be?' said Shaun.

'No, but I'm wondering whether Mario Genovese might know who he was, which might explain why our witness no longer wants to talk. It appears our victim had been in hiding for at least five years.' Stella looked at Shaun. 'He was impersonating someone he'd killed.'

'Sounds like a nice bloke.'

Stella smiled. 'The ladies at the retirement village where he was living thought so.'

'Are you going to ask Genovese?' said Shaun.

'What do you think, Inspector?' said Stella.

'Let's ask our witness first.'

***

Stella hated the Remand Centre. The place gave her the creeps. All the locked doors and security checks, and the hard sounds echoing through the place jarred every fibre of her body.

Johnnie Roach was waiting for them in the interview room on the first level. Stella thought Roach was an arsehole and had to take three deep breaths before opening the door to enter the interview room with Brian.

A corrections officer sat in the corner of the room. Roach was staring at the floor.

'Hello, Johnnie,' said Stella. She'd spent hours interviewing Roach as they'd tried to piece together the events around the brutal murders of three prostitutes in Mile End. In the end, when it looked like he was going to be pinned with the blame, Roach had agreed to testify against Mario Genovese to save his own skin. Now he was saying he'd killed them himself and that Genovese wasn't involved, despite the fact that he'd admitted to working for Genovese.

'What the fuck do you want? Didn't you get the message?'

Stella sat opposite Roach at the table, with Brian standing behind her. 'I was wondering why you changed your mind?'

Roach said nothing.

'Would it have anything to do with this bloke?' Stella slid a photograph of Bob across the table to Roach and watched his face.

Roach folded his arms across his chest. 'Who the fuck's that?'

'That's what I'd like to know?' said Stella. 'He claimed he was someone called Robert Cunningham but it turns out he wasn't. Now he's in the morgue with a bullet through his head. Do you know who he was?' Stella paused and waited. 'Is that why you changed your mind, Johnnie?'

'I've got nothing more to say.' Roach stood and looked at his guard.

After meeting with Roach, they moved to an interview room in the west wing of the Remand Centre to interview Mario Genovese in the company of his lawyer.

'Well, if it's not the lovely Stella Bruno. What brings you here, sweetheart?'

Stella knew he did it to press her buttons, but she still had to keep herself in check.

'Mr Genovese, I was wondering if you knew who this was.' Stella placed the photograph of Bob on the table.

Mario Genovese studied the photograph and then looked up. 'What makes you think I'd know who this is?'

'I'm asking everyone. Thought you might have missed seeing his photo on the news last night.'

'I saw it, sweetheart.' He shook his head. 'But, sorry, I've got no idea who he was.'

When they reached the car park, Stella turned to Brian. 'What do you think?'

'They lied to us.'

'That suggests our man must have had some connection with organised crime right here in Adelaide.'

'And, maybe they called in someone from Victoria to knock him off,' said Brian, as he opened the car.

If there was one thing Stella liked about summer, it was the balmy evenings spent outdoors eating under the pergola attached to her brother Stefano's house.

Eating together at night was a family tradition. During the summer months, they gathered around the table under the pergola to share their evening meal and talk about their day. In the winter months, they congregated in her parents' kitchen and took turns preparing the main meal. Her mother always made the dessert and her father, who regarded himself as a master barista, always made the coffee.

Family was important to Stella's parents, who had moved onto the two-acre block in Paradise that housed the family shortly after Stefano's birth. They'd built their home in the centre of the block and surrounded it with a working garden. When Stella and her brother had married, they had each built a house on opposite sides of the family home. The three houses shared a common yard where her father grew fruit and vegetables and raised chickens after spending his working day supervising the pouring of concrete on building sites all over the city.

Stella knew it was the close-knit nature of her family that had helped her survive the loss of her husband when their son was a five-year-old. If it hadn't been for her mother, she would never have been able to return to work. Her mother was just as much mother as grandmother to Josh. In fact, he was so close to her that his paternal grandmother had tried to buy his affection with expensive gifts. It was thanks to Rick's parents that Josh had every high-tech device a fourteen-year-old boy could wish for.

Stefano's wife Denise was Stella's closest friend, the one she shared her secrets with and who was there for her when she needed to pour her heart out. There were some things Stella didn't feel comfortable discussing with her mother.

Stella sat at the table she had finished setting. She could hear Josh playing table tennis with his cousin Paolo on the veranda while they waited for Stefano to finish barbecuing the meat for the night's meal. Josh and his cousin spent a lot of time together, seeing they were the same age, went to the same school and lived in the same compound. They even went to school together in the same car driven by their grandmother.

Stella's thoughts drifted to Shaun Porter. She didn't know why but she wondered when she'd see him again. There was something about him she found attractive and it wasn't just his disarming smile.

Denise placed a glass of white wine on the table in front of Stella and sat down.

'Who are you thinking about, Stella? I haven't seen that happy look on your face for a long time.'

Stella remembered that being a good cook wasn't Denise's only attribute. She was also very intuitive.

'I met a man at work today.'

'Oh? You meet men at work every day. What's so special about this one?'

Stella took a sip of the Chardonnay. 'I don't know how to describe it, Denise. There's something about him. I got a tingle up my arm when we shook hands.'

'Is that all?'

Stella looked at her sister-in-law. 'Thought I was going to faint. Lucky Frank asked me to sit down.' She laughed.

'Is this someone that clown knows?'

Her tone reminded Stella that Denise didn't approve of Frank Williams and the way he treated her. 'No. He's someone that works at the DPP I hadn't met before.'

'Does he have a name?'

'Shaun. Shaun Porter.' Stella felt her face getting hot.

Denise nudged her in the side. 'And what else do you know about him?'

Stella shrugged her shoulders. 'He's got nice blue eyes.'

They laughed.

'Nine years is long enough, don't you think? It's not right not having a man in your life.'

'I don't even know if this one is available.'

'Would you like him to be?'

Stella looked at her brother loading the cooked meat onto a plate. She missed Rick, but he wasn't coming back, and she wondered what Josh was missing out on not having a father figure in his life. Having access to his uncle and his grandfather was one thing, but she knew it wasn't the same as having a father. She wondered if she'd left it too long.

Denise nudged her again.

'I think so.'

'What are you two looking so wistful about?' said Stefano, as he put the cooked meat on the table.

'Stella's met a man,' said Denise.

'About bloody time,' said Stefano, grinning from ear to ear. 'Come on kids. Time to eat.'

CHAPTER 5

THE FOLLOWING Monday was a slow day. Stella did her admin tasks. Brian searched the files of the laptop they had found in Bob's apartment. They waited for a response to their public appeal for help in identifying who he was.

'Might have something here, Sarge.'

Stella looked up from her computer. Brian was still looking at the screen of Bob's laptop.

'I've found the details of a storage unit at Windsor Gardens in an email. And, there's a monthly payment going from his credit card to Storage King. Looks like he must have something in storage.'

Stella arranged for a warrant to authorise a search of the storage unit. Half an hour later they were standing in the office of the Storage King facility at Windsor Gardens.

'What unit was that again?' said the woman behind the counter, after she'd perused the search warrant.

'305,' said Stella.

'That's leased to a Mr Robert Cunningham. It's one of our smaller units. He's had stuff in storage with us for around five years.'

'Have you met him?' said Stella.

'I don't think so.'

Stella showed her the photograph Sheila McGregor had given them.

'Is that him?' The woman behind the counter looked up.

Stella nodded.

'I've seen him. He was here only a couple of weeks ago, on a Thursday I think. Drives a white Mitsubishi Lancer.'

'Yes, that sounds like him. His body was found in a white Lancer.'

'Was that Mr Cunningham that was shot at the Old Spot Hotel?'

'No, but it was someone claiming to be him. We don't know who he is yet but we do know he'd been impersonating Mr Cunningham for at least five years. Maybe whatever he's got in storage will tell us.'

'Oh.'

'How do people access their storage units?' said Stella.

'Everybody has a unique access code that operates the gate.'

'So, do you have a record of every time he came and went?'

'Oh, yes. It's all recorded.'

'How often did he visit?'

'Let me have a look.'

Stella examined the display of wrapping materials, storage boxes and padlocks on the wall behind the counter.

'Looks like he dropped in on the second Thursday of the month, every month.'

'Did he stay long?'

'About an hour by the look of it.'

'Okay. Can you show us where unit 305 is located?'

'Do you have the combination to his padlock?'

'We have a number we found in his paperwork but we've also got a Plan B.'

Brian held up the bolt cutter he'd bought along for the purpose of gaining entry into the unit.

After a short walk through a labyrinth of corridors, they were standing outside unit 305. Brian tried the combination he'd located in Bob's papers and the padlock clicked open. He lifted the roller door, and they stared into a room about the size of a small garden shed. It was empty except for a large metal trunk locked with a padlock.

Brian lifted the bolt cutter, fitted it around the shaft of the padlock and pulled the handles together. The shaft shattered, and the padlock dropped to the concrete floor with a thud.

Stella pulled on her latex gloves and lifted the lid of the trunk. The smell of oil on metal wafted into the air of the storage unit.

'Holy shit!' said Brian.

'Looks like our man could have started his own private war,' said Stella, closing the lid of the trunk on the weapons cache. 'Lock the door. We'll need to get some weapons handlers here to take care of this lot.'

They waited until the weapons specialists arrived and unpacked the trunk to discover that Bob had three high powered rifles, four handguns and several hundred rounds of ammunition stored in unit 305.

On Tuesday morning, Stella logged on to her computer and noticed she had an email from Crime Stoppers. She opened the email and read the contact details of a woman who wished to speak to her about the man in the photograph.

Stella called the mobile number listed in the email. 'Is that Sonya Richards?'

'Yes. Who's this?'

'Detective Sergeant Bruno. You left a message with Crime Stoppers for me to call.'

'Can we meet someplace?'

'Where do you have in mind?'

'I'll be in the city in about fifteen minutes. I'm on the train.'

'Would you like me to meet you at the station?' said Stella.

'How will I recognise you?' said Sonya.

'I'm wearing a navy blue skirt with a white top and I'll be with a tall man in a dark suit. What train are you on?'

'I'm on the train from Seaford that gets in at nine forty-six. I'm wearing a red blouse.'

'I'll meet you at the end of the platform. Okay?'

'Okay.'

Stella slipped her mobile into her handbag and stood. 'Brian, get your coat. We need to be at Adelaide Railway Station before nine forty-six.'

They arrived in the area at the end of the platforms as a woman wearing a red shirt and blue jeans came through the exit closest to North Terrace.

'Sonya Richards?' said Stella.

'Detective Sergeant Bruno?'

Stella held out her ID. 'Like a coffee?'

Sonya nodded and Stella guided her over to a table outside the Station Cafe while Brian went into the shop and ordered three coffees.

'I understand you wanted to talk about our mystery man,' said Stella, opening the image of Bob on her iPhone and showing it to Sonya.

'I think he might be my father,' said Sonya, as Brian arrived with the coffees.

'Want to elaborate?' said Stella.

'We haven't heard from him for years. We thought he was dead.'

'When was the last time you saw him?'

'At Mum's funeral.' Sonya added sugar to her coffee. 'She's been dead for six years. They'd been divorced for ten years when Mum died, and I'd only seen Dad a couple times since the divorce.'

'So, you weren't close?'

Sonya shook her head. 'He was a hard man. I don't know how Mum put up with him for as long as she did. He was always away somewhere interstate, and he drank a lot when he was home. He was a violent bastard at times, too.'

'What did your father do for a living?'

'He drove one of those overnight trucks interstate. We'd only see him once or twice a week if we were lucky. Some weeks, when I was a kid, he didn't come home at all.'

'What's your father's name?'

'Vince. Vince Reynolds.'

'Does he have any distinctive features that might help identify him?' said Stella.

'He's got a tattoo of a monkey here.' Sonya tapped the top of her right arm.

Stella cast her mind back to the autopsy. 'Is there anybody else who could identify him?'

'I guess my husband might be able to but he's in the RAH, which is why I'm in town. Silly bugger's had a heart attack.'

'Oh, I'm sorry to hear that,' said Stella. 'How is he?'

'The doctor says he'll survive, but he's going to have to change his diet and stop drinking so much red wine.'

Stella looked at Brian and smiled. Then she drained her coffee and waited for Sonya to finish hers. 'Are you up to a visit to the morgue? I think you might be right.'

Twenty minutes later they stood outside the viewing window in the police morgue. The attendant pulled back the sheet covering the body and revealed the black shape of a monkey on the upper right arm of the corpse.

Sonya looked at the body and then at Stella. 'That's him.'

The telephone on Stella's desk rang as she and Brian returned to the squad room after taking a statement from Sonya Richards.

'DS Bruno.'

'Got a minute to come down to Ballistics, Sergeant? I've got something for you.'

'Be right there.' Stella looked at Brian. 'That was Ballistics. Want to come for a walk?'

They caught the lift down to the lower level of the basement and made their way to the firing range used by Ballistics to test fire weapons.

'I test fired those guns you bought in from Windsor Gardens and ran the results through the database.' The ballistics analyst handed Stella a four-page report. 'We got four hits. One of the rifles was used to fire a round in a murder near Parkes, in New South Wales, and three of the handguns are connected to killings in Victoria. One in Melbourne, and two near Bendigo.'

Stella thanked the analyst and they made their way back upstairs.

'Sounds like our man might have been doing more than driving a truck,' said Stella.

'Guess we'd better ask if anyone interstate knows anything about this Vince Reynolds.'

'Perhaps I'd better talk to DI Williams. He likes doing that PR stuff with his mates interstate. Why don't you see if you can find someone at that trucking company Sonya mentioned that knows anything about Reynolds and where he went interstate?'

Stella knocked on the doorframe of DI Williams' office.

The Inspector looked up from his reading. 'What's up, Bruno?'

'Two things, sir. Our man has a name: Vince Reynolds. His daughter has identified the body and given us a statement.'

'Are you sure this woman is his daughter?' said DI Williams.

'I'll run a background check using the ID she gave me, but she knew about the tattoo.'

'What was the other thing?'

'I've just come from Ballistics. They've tested those guns we picked up from Windsor Gardens and four of them are on the national database.' She dropped the four-page report on his desk. 'The details are in here.'

The inspector picked up the report and scanned its contents. 'Looks like he's been a busy boy.'

'Well, we don't know whether he was the shooter or the weapons handler, but given that the pistol he had in his apartment was used to kill Cunningham, I'm guessing he was the shooter.' Stella waited.

'That's probably something we're not going to resolve. It's not as if we can ask him, is it?'

Stella shook her head. 'Do you want to liaise with Sydney and Melbourne, or do you want me to do that?'

'I'll do it, but I want you to confirm this woman is who she says she is before we break the news to them.'

Stella returned to her desk. Brian had gone to lunch. She sat down, intending to call the Office of the Registrar of Births, Deaths and Marriages to join the dots between Sonya Richards and Vince Reynolds, when her mobile phone rang.

'DS Bruno.'

'Hi, Stella. It's Shaun, Shaun Porter.'

Stella felt her heart skip a beat. 'What can I do for you, Shaun?'

'I was wondering if you were available to join me for a quick lunch.'

Stella looked at her watch. It was just after one o'clock. She decided she could use a break and having one with Shaun might be fun. It would certainly be a change from having lunch with Brian or alone. 'Where are you?'

'I'm downstairs. We could nick around to Cibo in Hutt Street if you've got time.'

'I'd like that. See you in a couple of minutes.'

She grabbed her handbag and went to make sure she was presentable before heading downstairs.

Shaun was standing in the foyer of Police Headquarters, chatting with the security officer guarding the entrance, when Stella emerged from the lift. His face lit up when he noticed her coming through the security barrier.

'This is a bit of a surprise,' said Stella.

'I was just passing and thought I'd try my luck. I'm on my way back to the office from Holden Hill.'

'I'm glad you did. Are we walking?'

'I've got a car outside. Shouldn't be too hard to find a park in Halifax Street.'

Ten minutes later they were sitting at an outside table in Hutt Street reading the menu and deciding what to eat.

Stella decided on the Insalata Mista. Shaun ordered the Baguette Arrosto di Manzo, and they opted to share a large bottle of San Pellegrino Sparkling Mineral Water.

They looked at each other across the table.

'I hope you don't think I'm being too forward but I haven't been able to stop thinking about you since the other day,' said Shaun.

Stella felt the heat of a blush sweep across her cheeks.

'I'm sorry, I didn't mean to embarrass you,' said Shaun.

'That's the nicest thing a man's said to me in a long time, Shaun.' Stella smiled and touched his hand. 'So, tell me a bit about yourself. How long have you been with the DPP?'

'Nearly three months. I was with Public Prosecutions in Melbourne before that.'

'Oh, what made you come to Adelaide?'

'My daughter got into law at Adelaide. I wasn't ready to let her come on her own.'

Stella noted the 'my daughter' and took a sip of her mineral water as the waiter delivered their meals.

'Sarah took it pretty hard losing her mother.'

'When was that?' said Stella, hoping it wasn't too recent.

'A little over three years ago.'

'I'm sorry,' said Stella. 'I know what that feels like. I lost my husband nine years ago.'

'That must have been hard, losing him at a young age.'

Stella rested her fork on the side of her plate. 'How old do you think I am, Shaun?'

Shaun smiled. She felt her heart melting.

'You don't honestly think I'm going the answer that question, do you?'

Stella laughed. 'I have a fourteen-year-old son, so I'm not that young, even if I look it.'

'What's his name?'

'Josh.'

'Does he look anything like you?'

Stella shook her head. 'He's the spitting image of his father. What about your daughter, Sarah?'

'Poor kid looks like me.' Shaun bit into his baguette.

'Where are you living?' said Stella.

'We're renting. I found a two-bedroom apartment in Rowlands Place.'

'That must be convenient for work. I live out at Paradise. Takes me at least half an hour to drive in, sometimes even longer.'

Shaun chuckled. 'Adelaide people have no idea what a long commute is. It used to take me more than an hour to get into work on the train in Melbourne. Now I walk to work and Sarah either catches the tram or walks to uni. It's great. We're right next door to the market, too.'

'So, you're into cooking, then?'

Shaun refilled their glasses with mineral water. 'I'm tempted to eat out, especially with all those eating places in Gouger Street but,' he tapped his hand on his belly, 'it's not good for the waist line. Besides, Sarah doesn't like eating out much.'

'Did you cook before your wife died or is this a new skill?'

'I worked in the kitchen of a place like this when I was studying. Started washing pots and pans and ended up as the chef's offsider, so I had something to fall back on when Cathy died.'

Shaun looked at his watch. 'I have to get going. I've got a two o'clock appointment.'

'I'm done.'

'Do you think we could do this again? I'd like to get to know you, Stella. I like your energy.'

'I'd like that, Shaun. Maybe next time we could try one of those restaurants in Gouger Street for an evening meal after work.'

'When are you available?'

'You don't waste any time, Mr Porter.'

'We never know what's going to happen, Stella. Life is full of surprises and I like to seize the good ones.'

'What about tomorrow night, then?'

'Okay, shall we say six thirty at Gaucho's?'

'Sounds good to me. I'll meet you there.'

They walked around the corner from Hutt Street to where they'd left the car in Halifax Street. Not wanting to sound like a love-struck school girl, Stella decided it might be a good idea to talk about work. 'Have you heard the name Vince Reynolds in connection with any unsolved murders in Victoria, Shaun?'

'Doesn't ring any bells. Why?'

'That's the name of my mystery man. I don't know if you've heard, but we found some guns he had in storage. Three of them are connected to murders in Victoria.'

'Where?'

'Two near Bendigo. One in Melbourne.'

'Do you remember when?'

'The one in Melbourne was in 1991 and the two near Bendigo were in 2004.'

'I don't recall the Melbourne killing but I remember the Bendigo case. There were two bodies in a shallow grave about five kilometres from Bendigo. The police believed they'd been shot elsewhere and dumped there. I'm pretty sure they were gangland figures.'

'Well, we might have their killer in the morgue. Funny thing is, though, the weapon used to kill him was used in another gangland murder in Melbourne a couple of years ago.'

'Sounds like someone might have known who was behind those Bendigo killings, Stella.'

It took almost thirty minutes for the Office of the Registrar of Births, Deaths and Marriages to ring back and confirm that Sonya Richards, nee Reynolds, born on the 28th day of August 1976, was the daughter of Vincent James and Margaret Helen Reynolds.

Stella listened in as Brian spoke to someone at the trucking company Sonya had told them her father had worked for.

'Okay. I'll bring a photograph.' Brian hung up.

'What's their story, Brian?'

'They don't have a record of anyone called Vince or Vincent Reynolds working for them but that doesn't mean he didn't work for them more than ten years ago. He suggested I visit with a photograph. One of their dispatchers, a woman called Regina Wild, has been there since Adam was a boy and, apparently, she has a good memory for faces. If that doesn't work, he said we were welcome to look through their paper records.'

The drive to the office of Interstate Overnight, on Sir Donald Bradman Drive in Cowandilla, took a little over fifteen minutes, thanks to the traffic heading towards the airport at West Beach.

Stella stood with her arms crossed as Brian introduced himself to the office manager and asked to speak to Regina Wild.

'Take a seat. I'll get her for you.' The office manager disappeared through the door into the warehouse where people were loading parcels into the back of several trucks. When he returned, he was accompanied by a short, overweight, grey-haired woman wearing silver rimmed glasses.

'How can I help you, love?'

'We want to know if this man has ever worked here.' Brian placed a print of the photograph of Bob that Sheila McGregor had given them on the counter.

Regina picked up the photograph and peered at it over the top of her glasses and then held it out at arm's-length and looked at it through her glasses.

'I remember him. One of the few that had any manners. Not like most of the clowns that work here. I'd say he quit about ten years ago. At least, he stopped turning up for work.' She handed the photograph back to Brian.

'Do you remember his name?' said Stella.

'Roach. Jack Roach.'

Shit, thought Stella. He'd be old enough to be Johnnie's father.

'Do you remember someone called Vince Reynolds, at all?' said Stella.

'No-one by that name's worked here in my time, love, and I've been here since 1976.'

Stella turned to the office manager. 'Do you have a record of this Jack Roach?'

'Let me have a look. It'll be a paper file if we still have one.'

They waited while the office manager searched through several folders in his filing cabinet.

'Here it is, and it looks like we have a copy of his driver's licence.' He handed the file to Stella.

Stella looked at the photograph of Jack Roach and then at the photograph of Bob. 'What do you think, Brian?'

'Looks like a younger version of our man to me.'

'Can we have a copy of this?'

'Take the file. It's of no use to me,' said the office manager.

Back at the office, Brian scanned the copy of Jack Roach's driver's licence to convert it into a digital image. Then, he sent the image to their photographic experts, along with the image he'd emailed to himself from Sheila McGregor's iPhone, and asked them to confirm if the images were of the same person.

CHAPTER 6

As soon as she arrived home from work, Stella went to find Denise. She didn't even stop by her mother's to see Josh.

'Guess what happened to me today.'

Denise stopped cutting up the salad she was preparing. 'Going by that stupid grin on your face, I'd say you've seen him.'

Stella pirouetted and twirled her skirt. 'Shaun took me to lunch.'

Denise put down her knife. 'Just like that? You only met him the other day.'

Stella hugged her sister-in-law and kissed her on the cheek. 'He just called out of the blue and asked if I'd join him for lunch.'

'Where'd you go?'

'Cibo, in Hutt Street.'

Denise frowned. 'That doesn't sound very romantic.'

'And, he's asked me to dinner tomorrow night, at Gaucho's.'

'Are you going?'

Stella grinned. 'What do you think? Of course, I'm going.'

Denise hugged her again. 'I'm so happy for you. Tell me all about it. What did he say?'

Stella sat on the stool while Denise returned to her salad

making. 'Said he couldn't stop thinking about me after we'd met the other day.'

'He's fallen hook, line and sinker, then?'

'I wasn't even fishing.'

'Some part of you was fishing, honey, and it looks like you've reeled one in. What was it you said the other day about that tingling in your arm when he shook your hand?' Denise shook her head. 'Really, Stella, you need to pay more attention to what's going on inside you, and be careful what you wish for.' She laughed. 'So, what's his story? Is he someone you want to get mixed up with?'

'He's got the most gorgeous blue eyes, Denise. I feel like I'm melting inside when he looks at me, especially when he smiles.'

'Think we need a drink,' said Denise. She walked over to the fridge and took out a bottle of Chardonnay. 'Want to get a couple of glasses from that tray over there on the bench?'

Stella placed two wine glasses on the table and Denise poured them each a drink.

'Here's to happy days!'

Stella lifted her glass and clinked it against Denise's. 'I'll drink to that!'

'When are you going to tell Mum?'

'I guess I'll have to tell her tonight, unless I spin her a story about why I'll be late home tomorrow.'

'You know that won't work. What about Josh? What are you going to tell him?'

'That I'm having dinner with a new friend. It's too early to tell him anything else, don't you think?'

Denise nodded in agreement. 'So, what did you find out about Shaun?'

Stella smiled. 'He's available.'

They burst into giggles and it was several minutes before they could continue.

'What else did you find out?' said Denise, wiping tears from her eyes.

'He has a nineteen-year-old daughter doing first year law at Adelaide,' said Stella.

'What's her name?'

'Sarah.'

'That's nice. Where is he living?'

'He's renting an apartment in Rowlands Place.'

'That's that new block of apartments near the Central Market, isn't it?'

Stella nodded and took a sip of Chardonnay. 'He's only been here three months. That's why I hadn't seen him before.'

'Where was he before?'

'In Melbourne.'

'What's the story with this Sarah's mother?'

'She died around three years ago. He didn't go into the details.'

They sat looking at each other.

'I hope this works out, Denise. He feels so right,' said Stella.

'Let it happen, honey. If it's meant to be it will work out.'

Stella stood. 'Perhaps I'd better go and tell Mum.'

By ten o'clock Wednesday morning, Stella knew Vince Reynolds and Jack Roach were the same person. She closed the email with the results of the analysis of the images Brian had forwarded to her and called the Remand Centre.

Shortly after eleven o'clock, Stella and Brian were sitting in a sterile interview room in the Remand Centre with Johnnie Roach.

Stella placed the hard copies of the photographs she had brought with her face down on the table.

'Tell me about your father, Johnnie.'

'Why would I want to do that?'

Stella flipped over the copy of Jack Roach's driver's licence. 'This him?'

Johnnie grabbed onto the table to stop himself falling backwards out of his chair. 'Where did you get that?'

'From the place where he worked.'

Johnnie looked at Brian and then at Stella. 'He drove a truck.'

'I know that much, Johnnie. They told us he drove a truck interstate. Mostly overnight runs to Sydney or Melbourne. When was the last time you saw him?'

Johnnie looked down at his hands and shifted in his seat. 'I haven't seen him for about ten years.'

Stella almost felt sorry for him. 'What sort of father was he?'

'One of those absent ones. I lived with me mum before coming over here to work.'

'Oh, where did you live before coming to Adelaide?'

'Bendigo.'

Stella looked at Brian and then turned her attention back to Johnnie. 'How come you haven't seen your father for, what was it, ten years?'

Johnnie shrugged his shoulders. 'He told me he had to disappear and not to come looking for him.'

'Must have been a bit of a surprise to see his face on the TV the other night?' Stella flipped over the photograph of Bob. 'We've had these photos digitally compared. They're of the same person.'

'I know,' said Johnnie.

'Why didn't you tell us that the last time we were here?'

'It's complicated.'

'Try me.'

'You know who I work for. Well, Dad might have been driving a truck for someone else but he worked for them, too.'

'That why he had to disappear?'

'He wanted to retire, but it wasn't that simple.'

Stella leant back in her chair and crossed her arms in front of her breasts. 'Did you know about his guns?'

'Who do you think taught me how to use one?'

'Do you know what he did with them?'

Johnnie shook his head. 'I never asked.'

Stella doubted that was the truth. 'Did you know you have a half-sister?'

Johnnie sat back in his chair. 'What are you talking about?'

'Seems your absent father had a second family and another name. He was also known as Vince Reynolds.'

'You're pulling my leg, aren't you?'

'Your sister identified the body as being her father. Only she knew him as Vince Reynolds. She was the one that told us he drove trucks interstate. That's how we got this.' Stella tapped the copy of Jack Roach's driver's licence. 'My loose ends now, Johnnie, are that your father's weapons are linked to several murders interstate, and I need to find out who killed him. Got any ideas?'

'Wish I could help you, Sergeant, but I can't. If I say anything to you... well you know how the game's played.'

Stella and Brian stood next to their car outside the Remand Centre.

'We need to look into the details of those interstate killings, Sarge. Sounds like someone worked out our man was responsible and hunted him down, probably with the help of Facebook.'

'Let's hope DI Williams has been earning his money, then,' said Stella. 'Come on, open her up. It's too bloody hot to be standing out here.'

When Stella reported what she'd learnt from Johnnie Roach to DI Williams, the inspector had some news of his own to share.

'Victoria Police think the three murders linked to our man's guns are connected. The victims all worked for the Franzon network, which was heavily into methamphetamine distribution across the eastern states. Most of the big players are still doing time but some of their operatives have been released over the last few years.'

'Roach told us his father worked for the Genovese group. I'm guessing that would be Mario's father,' said Stella, 'seeing that he's been in hiding for the last ten years.'

'Sounds like our man could have been a hitman for Genovese, using the interstate trucking job as his cover,' said DI Williams.

Stella thought that sounded feasible. 'So, I wonder who found out where he was. Genovese's people or someone connected to these Franzon people?' said Stella.

'I asked about that other murder in Victoria, the one connected to the weapon used to kill our victim,' said DI Williams. 'Turns out the victim of that shooting worked for a rival gang that stepped into the meth trade when Franzon was shut down. Suggests to me, Bruno, that our killer might be someone connected to the old Franzon network who's settling scores.'

Stella nodded. 'Did they give you the names of the Franzon people that are back on the street, sir?'

'They sent through some photographs. The only one that's disappeared from their radar is this woman.' He turned his monitor so Stella could she the image. 'Her name's Donna Brewer. She was the partner of one of the Bendigo victims.'

'What was she in for?'

'She's one of Franzon's daughters. Brewer is her married name. She was running the operation in Bendigo.'

'Definitely someone with motive, then,' said Stella.

'See if you can connect her with our victim. Not much point having someone with motive but no opportunity, Bruno.'

Stella nodded. 'Learn anything from Sydney, sir?'

'Pretty much the same story. They identified the victim as one of Franzon's couriers.'

'Send me that photograph, sir. I've got someone who might be able to tell me if she's been around looking for Bob Cunningham.'

Stella used the drive to Gawler to review her case notes while Brian dealt with the traffic and navigation. When she finished reading her notes, she looked up to see a red car zip in front of them and draw away into the distance.

'How fast do you reckon he's going, Brian?'

'I'm sitting on the limit, so he must be doing at least a hundred and twenty.'

'Guess he's lucky you haven't got one of those pursuit licences.'

Brian glanced at her. 'I'm too old for that much excitement.'

'Come on, Brian. You're never too old for anything.'

'Can you come around and talk to May? She's always telling me I'm too old for something.'

Stella laughed.

'I'll be lucky if get to do anything in my retirement, presuming I live that long.'

'How's the golf going?'

'Good. I'm really enjoy it. It's been ages since I got up that early for anything. Surprising how quick you get back into the swing of it.'

'What about the diet? How's that going?'

'Yeah, well that's not quite as easy to get used to. I feel like a school kid eating my lunch these days, even if it's supposed to be good for me.'

'You're lucky May makes your lunch for you. A lot of wives wouldn't.'

'So she keeps telling me. Hey, what do you know?' Brian pointed to his left as he slowed the car to pass a patrol car with flashing lights parked behind the red car that had passed them earlier.

Stella looked across at the driver and shook her head. 'I was wrong, Brian. The idiot's a woman.'

Brian pulled into the car park outside the Community Centre at the Vineyard Retirement Village and they walked over to James Murphy's apartment.

'Don't mind these twenty-eight days,' said Stella, looking up into the clear blue sky.

'Sure as hell beats those forty plus days,' said Brian, as he stepped onto the porch and rang the doorbell of unit 46.

There was no answer.

'Didn't we make an appointment, Sarge?'

As Stella was reaching for her iPhone, the door of unit 44 opened and James Murphy emerged into the sunshine.

Stella showed him the photographs of Donna Brewer supplied by Victoria Police.

'Is this the woman you saw knocking on Bob's door?'

'You mean, is she the district nurse?'

'Could she be?'

James Murphy studied the photographs. 'Possibly. She was wearing sun glasses and her hair was different, but there is something about her overall appearance that reminds me of her. Does that help?'

'I'm pretty sure that wouldn't hold up in court, Mr Murphy, but it confirms my suspicions about who may have killed Bob.'

Stella spent Thursday afternoon going over her notes from the Genovese investigation, since the DPP had not yet withdrawn the charges, and the case was due in court the following day.

At six o'clock, she stopped reading and freshened up, and then drove herself down into the vicinity of Gaucho's and parked her car in the Central Market car park.

Shaun was standing at the bar talking to the bartender when she entered the restaurant.

'I have a table in the other room,' he said, as she joined him. 'Do you want a drink?'

'I'll have a mineral water, thanks.'

'I'll bring your drinks to your table, sir,' said the bartender.

Shaun led her through to the rear section of the restaurant, to a table with a view of the small courtyard in one direction and of a wall covered with large posters explaining that a gaucho was an Argentinian cowboy in another.

'It's a while since I've eaten here,' said Stella, as she sat down.

'I'm a red meat man, so I've been here a few times since we moved in down the street.'

A waiter appeared with their drinks and the menus. He explained the specials and said he'd come back to take their order.

'Shall we start with the sourdough?' said Shaun.

'Okay. Then, I think I'll have the Cordero, the lamb cutlets,' said Stella. 'What are you having?'

'The Bife de Chorizo sounds inviting. I enjoy a good steak.'

Stella read the entry for Bife de Chorizo. '400 grams sounds like a big piece of meat.'

'I didn't get time for lunch today.' Shaun looked around before continuing. 'Genovese starts in the morning. Spent the day going over everything to work out if we could proceed without our star witness taking the stand. Interested in sharing a salad?'

'The Ensalada Pera looks nice. What did you decide?'

'The boss thinks we still have a chance. It comes down to which version of Roach's story we can get the jury to believe. Anyway, that's enough about work. Let's talk about something more interesting.'

'What do you have in mind?'

'You.'

Stella felt a little self-conscious and surprised that she couldn't feel herself blushing.

The waiter arrived and took their order. 'And, what would you like to drink?'

'I'll stay with the mineral water,' said Stella.

'I'll have glass of the Bodega Malbec,' said Shaun.

'See you're getting into the atmosphere with an Argentinian wine,' said Stella, as the waiter collected the menus and walked towards the kitchen.

'It's a nice change from a Shiraz.'

'I'm a white wine girl when I'm having a glass,' said Stella, sipping her mineral water, 'but I rarely drink when I'm out. Wouldn't look too good on my record being busted for DUI.'

'Well, I'm walking home,' said Shaun, 'so I guess I could have a few, but one glass will be enough, especially before a day in court. So, what do you do when you're not at work?'

Stella felt herself relax in the glow of his friendly smile. 'Being a mother takes up a fair amount of my free time.'

'Know what you mean. At least Sarah is old enough to look after herself. How old did you say your son was?'

The waiter arrived with their sourdough bread and side dishes of extra virgin olive oil and organic sea salt.

'Josh is fourteen. He's at that age where all he wants to do is play sport. Just as well my mother is a hard task master, otherwise he'd never get his homework done,' Stella smiled. It felt good sharing bits of her life with Shaun.

'Does your mother live near you?'

'Across the courtyard.'

'That sounds pretty convenient.'

'Josh was only five when his father was killed.' Stella gazed into Shaun's deep blue eyes. 'If it hadn't been for my parents, I wouldn't have been able to stay on the job. Did you get any support when you wife died?'

Shaun shook his head. 'Cathy was English. Her folks live outside London. Mine are here in South Australia, which is another reason I came back to Adelaide.'

'Oh, so you're a local boy?'

'I grew up in Clare. That's where my father had his law practice until he retired.'

'Do your parents still live in Clare?' said Stella, dipping a piece of the sourdough bread into the olive oil before placing it into her mouth.

'Dad wanted to retire down here but Mum won't leave her friends, so they're still there.' Shaun smiled. 'I never understood why he wanted to leave.'

The waiter arrived with their main meal and they shifted their focus to eating.

At eight thirty, Shaun walked Stella to her car. 'We must do this again.'

'Yes. I enjoyed it.'

'Guess I'll see you tomorrow, in court.' Shaun shut her door and walked off towards the stairwell.

Think I'd like to see more of you, Mr Porter, Stella thought to herself as she watched him go.

CHAPTER 7

STELLA SPENT most of Friday in the Supreme Court building, first waiting to be called to testify, and then spending half an hour on the stand presenting her evidence to the court.

For Stella, it was an interesting experience being interviewed by Shaun, in his role as public prosecutor, and then having to stand her ground when Genovese's lawyer did his best to discredit her evidence.

When she got back to the office, Brian was waiting for her.

'How did it go?'

'The usual shit. Genovese's lawyer basically called me a liar and accused me of fabricating the evidence connecting his client to the murders.'

'You don't look too annoyed about it.'

Stella shrugged her shoulders and sat down. 'We've done our bit, Brian. It's up to the jury to decide now.'

'I hear the new boy at the DPP is running the case. What's he like?'

Stella knew there was no way she could lie to Brian. He could read her like a book.

'Actually, he's very nice, Brian. I had dinner with him last night.'

'I heard.'

Stella felt her face heating up.

Brian chuckled. 'You need to remember Adelaide's a small place, Sarge.'

Stella felt her face cooling as her blush retreated and was relieved when Brian changed the subject.

'That stolen RDNS car has turned up. Forensics are giving it the once over.'

'Oh, where was it found?'

'In the Riverbank car park. One of the attendants noticed it hadn't been moved for a week and called it in. And, there's something else I think we might want to look into.'

'What's that, Brian?'

'I was reading the case notes while you were in court.' He looked at Stella. 'I'm surprised we didn't notice it the other day when DI Williams gave us the information on Donna Brewer.'

'Oh shit!' said Stella, as it dawned on her what Brian was talking about. 'The name of the lad that found the body at the Old Spot.'

'Yes. I'm waiting for Victoria to confirm if she has a son or not.'

'Good work, Brian.'

When Stella arrived in the office on Monday morning, Brian was waiting for her.

'You're early, Brian.'

'Golf this morning. Wanted to be finished before it got too hot.'

'I heard the forecast. Hope we aren't spending too much time outside today.'

'Think we might be going out to the Old Spot. Donna Brewer

has a twenty-six-year-old son named Matthew Leonardo Brewer.'
He handed her a copy of the birth certificate Victoria Police had
sent through.

'We have his home address, don't we?' said Stella. 'Perhaps
we can get to him before he goes to work.'

Forty minutes later, they were standing outside the front door
of the house in Salisbury Park that Matt Brewer had given as his
home address, waiting for someone to respond to their knocking.
They were just about to leave when a young woman wearing a T-
shirt, and little else, opened the door rubbing her eyes.

'This better be bloody important!'

'Police,' said Stella, holding out her ID.

The woman crossed her arms. 'What do you want?'

'We're looking for Matt. He told us this was where he lived.'

'The shit's pissed off. Bastard didn't even leave me any
money for the rent.'

'When was the last time you saw him?'

'What day is it?'

'Monday,' said Brian.

'His stuff was gone when I got home from work last
Wednesday.'

'And you had no idea he was going to leave?'

She shook her head. 'Guess I should have seen it coming.
He'd been acting a bit strange ever since he found that dead bloke
at the pub.'

'In what way?' said Stella.

'He was always looking around as if someone was watching
him. Wanted to quit his job. Promised me he'd get another one
before he did. Said he couldn't stand to work there anymore.'

'So, are you his girlfriend?' said Stella.

'Not anymore!'

'How about you get dressed and we sit down and take a
statement?'

After taking a statement and several images of Matthew Brewer from his abandoned girlfriend, Stella and Brian called on the manager of the Old Spot Hotel.

'I haven't seen him since he signed off last Wednesday. Called his home number when he didn't show up for work on Thursday. His girlfriend said he'd cleared out, and she didn't know where he was or if he was coming back.'

'How long has he worked here?' said Stella.

'Couple of years. It's hard to keep these young blokes for much longer than that. They all seem to be in a hurry to get to somewhere else.'

'How was he after finding the body in the car park?'

'Just got on with his job as far as I could tell. He certainly didn't discuss it with me after he'd spoken to you.'

Stella showed the manager her photographs of Donna Brewer. 'Notice this woman in the hotel at all?'

'Can't say I have. Who is she?'

'Matt's mother,' said Stella. 'We think she may have visited him recently.'

'He never said anything about her to me.'

They were driving back to the city from the Old Spot Hotel when Stella's mobile phone rang.

'DS Bruno.'

'Sergeant, we lifted some prints from that RDNS car found at Riverbank. They match the set Victoria sent through for Donna Brewer.'

Stella relayed the news to Brian.

'That links her to the visit at the retirement village but we still don't have a link with the crime scene,' said Brian.

'Maybe she's not the shooter. What if it was Matt?' said Stella.

They sat in silence for a few moments.

'He doesn't have an alibi going by what his girlfriend told us,' said Brian. 'She was on night shift at the hospital that night according to her statement, so I guess he could have gone back to the hotel and waited in the car park for Bob to come out.'

Stella pulled the on-board computer towards her and ran a query on Matthew Brewer. 'He's clean. We've got nothing on him.'

'Victoria told me the same thing,' said Brian.

'We need to get his photo and a description of his car circulated.'

Stella queried the Motor Vehicle Registration database with Brewer's name and address details. The computer displayed: 2014 Nissan Juke; Black; S891-ATS.

By the time they'd reached the intersection of Main North and Grand Junction Roads at Gepps Cross, Stella had issued an APB with two images of Matthew Brewer, a description of his car, and a warning that he might be armed and dangerous.

When they were back in the office, Stella relayed the content of the APB to Victoria Police and requested help with locating Donna Brewer, whose last known address was in Bendigo.

Stella's mobile phone rang as she returned to her desk from attending DI Williams' morning briefing. She fished it out of her handbag and glanced at the display. Although she didn't recognise the number, she accepted the call.

'DS Bruno.'

'Hi, Stella. Simon Murray from Elizabeth. Matt Brewer has just walked into the station. He wants to talk to you.'

Stella felt a wave of relief sweep through her and wondered why he'd turned himself in.

'Did he come in with a lawyer, Simon?'

'No. He's on his own.'

Maybe he's not the killer, thought Stella, wondering what he'd have to say for himself after disappearing without telling anyone.

'Okay. Hold him. I'm on my way.'

Stella ended the call and looked around for Brian, who had gone to get their morning coffees from the shop downstairs. While she waited for him to return, she called DI Williams' number.

'Thought you might like to know Matt Brewer has turned himself in at Elizabeth, sir. I'm on my way to interview him.'

'Keep me posted, Bruno.'

Brian arrived with two takeaway coffees as she was ending the call.

'Leave the lids on, Brian. We're going to Elizabeth. Matt Brewer has turned himself in.'

Thirty-five minutes later they were sitting in an interview room within the Elizabeth Police Complex with Matt Brewer, who looked like he hadn't had a decent night's sleep in a week.

'Want to start at the beginning, Matt?' said Stella.

Matt looked down at the table. 'I'm not sure where the beginning is.'

'How about why you decided to clear out without telling your girlfriend? She's worried sick about you.'

'I got scared.'

'What were you scared of?'

Matt shrugged his shoulders. 'I didn't know what to do when I worked out who'd killed the man in the car park.' He looked across the table at Stella through bloodshot eyes.

Stella thought she could see more pain than fear. 'Who do you think shot him, Matt?'

'My mum.'

With those words in her ears, Stella understood the pain behind his eyes. 'What makes you think that?'

'About three months ago, she sent me a photograph of him and said he was the man that had murdered my father. She'd heard he was living somewhere around Gawler and wanted to know if I'd seen him. When I told her I hadn't, she asked me to keep an eye out for him and let her know if I saw him anywhere.'

'And did you?'

'I promised I'd let her know if I did. Then I didn't think about. I just let it go. To be honest, I couldn't work out how she knew he'd killed Dad.'

Stella stayed silent and let him continue.

'Then, a few weeks ago we went to the pub for dinner one night and there he was. When we got home, I called my mother.'

'Do you know where your mother is?'

Matt shook his head.

'When was the last time you saw her?'

'Around three years ago, when she got out of prison.'

'So, you're not close?'

'My mother is not the sort of person I like to hang around with, Sergeant. She scares the shit out of me.'

'How old were you when your father was killed, Matt?'

'Fourteen.'

Stella thought of Josh.

'And, when your mother went to prison?'

'I was seventeen. That's when I came over here. We lost everything. The house, all the cars, all the money in the bank. It was all confiscated as the proceeds of crime. I had to start over on my own. They fucked up my life. I didn't even get to finish school.'

'So how did your mother make contact with you?'

'Called me on my mobile and then emailed me a photo.'

'Do you have her mobile number?'

'She's not answering the one she gave me. All you get is voice mail.'

Stella handed him her pen. 'Write it down for me.'

Matt wrote the number onto her notepad. 'What happens now?'

'Are you friends with her on Facebook?'

'I don't think she's on Facebook. At least, not under her own name. I've looked.'

'Where have you been for the last few days, Matt?'

'I crashed at a friend's place. I didn't know where else to go.'

'Can I have the details, please? We'll want to check that out.'

Matt gave her the name and contact details of his friend.

'Have you been in touch with your girlfriend?'

Matt shook his head.

'I think you should give her a call. Might be a good idea to go home.' Stella smiled at him. 'And, I think your boss would appreciate a call, especially if you want to keep your job.'

'You mean I'm not in trouble?'

'You might be charged with hindering our enquiries but, for the time being, you're free to go as long as you promise me you'll go home. If I have to search for you again, I'll have you locked up. Understood?'

'I'm sorry, I panicked. I didn't mean to cause any trouble. I feel so guilty that I helped her kill him.'

'I'm not so sure he was that innocent himself, Matt. He may very well have killed your father and several other people.'

'Still doesn't make it right, though, does it?'

They got into the car for the trip back to the city from Elizabeth.

'If his calls are going through to voice mail, that number must still be active,' said Brian. 'We might be able to at least find out who it belongs to even if she's switched her phone off.'

'You chase that up. I want to know how she got access to Sheila's photo of Bob on Facebook.'

'That could be a hard one, Sarge. Either she's managed to friend Sheila or one of her friends. I don't think you can just discover photographs on Facebook unless the person has it up in a public profile.'

'We're half way to Gawler. Let me give Sheila McGregor a call and see if she's home. Perhaps we can have a look at her list of Facebook friends.'

'Worth a try, I suppose,' said Brian.

Twenty minutes later they were sitting in front of Sheila's laptop reviewing her list of friends on Facebook.

'Anybody in this list you don't know in the flesh?' said Brian.

'Most of them are people I know. A few are people I haven't seen since school days.'

'How did you find them?' said Stella.

'Oh, I don't know how to find friends. They find me and I just accept their invitations if I think I know them.'

'Get any new friend requests in the last three or four months?' said Brian.

Sheila looked at the list and pointed to the name of Elisabeth Greene. 'I haven't seen Liz since we finished high school. Her family moved to Victoria. Last time I heard from her was when she was getting married. Sent me an invitation but I couldn't go. Got quite a shock when she popped up on Facebook.'

Brian clicked on the link to see Elizabeth Greene's timeline. 'Not much activity. She hardly posts anything.'

'A few of my friends are like that,' said Sheila. 'Sometimes I wonder why they're on Facebook.'

'If they're not people you're really familiar with, Mrs McGregor, you might want to unfriend them,' said Brian. 'They could be people just wanting to get information from you.'

'Oh, I never thought of that.'

'Is Greene her married name?' said Stella.

'No, that's her maiden name. She married some bloke called Brewer in Bendigo.'

When they were back in the office, it took Brian an hour to establish that an Elizabeth Greene had married a Harold Brewer in Bendigo in 1965, and that their son Robert was the slain husband of Donna Brewer and the father of Matt. The same Elizabeth Brewer had died in a car accident in 2003.

'Bloody small world, Brian,' said Stella. 'Have we heard back from Telstra?'

'Let me check.' Brian opened his email. 'Number belongs to an Elizabeth Greene, with an address in Bendigo. It's been switched off since the day Bob was shot but the GPS data shows it was being used in Bathurst when she called Matt's number.'

'Shit! We're looking in the wrong place.'

CHAPTER 8

Four days after receiving South Australia's extradition warrant, New South Wales Police detained Donna Brewer in Bathurst, where she had been living under the name of Elizabeth Greene. She denied any connection to the murder of a man in the car park of the Old Spot Hotel in South Australia and to the unauthorised use of the RDNS vehicle abandoned in the Riverbank car park.

Acting on the details Stella had provided with the warrant, the arresting officers searched Brewer's house. They uncovered a smartphone and a 9mm Glock handgun, which they asked their weapons expert to test fire. The ballistic profile of the round fired matched the profile of the round that had killed Bob Cunningham.

When they opened the Facebook App on the smartphone, they discovered that Elizabeth Greene was friends with Sheila McGregor. After a little more searching, they located the copy of the photo of Bob she had downloaded from Sheila's timeline into her camera roll and then shared with her son.

During the extradition hearing in Bathurst, Brewer maintained her innocence, but the Magistrate agreed she had a case to answer and approved her extradition to South Australia to face charges.

A week after being arrested, Donna Brewer found herself in residence at the Adelaide Women's Prison, awaiting trial for the murder of Vince Reynolds, also known as Jack Roach and Robert Cunningham.

***

On the night that Donna Brewer was settling into the Adelaide Women's Prison, Stella was celebrating at Georges on Waymouth with Shaun, Brian and DI Williams.

'Here's to a job well done,' said DI Williams, raising his pint of beer above the dinner table.

'I'll drink to that,' said Shaun.

'I'm starting to think you'll drink to anything,' said Stella, smiling in Shaun's direction.

'Are you on the wagon?' said DI Williams, when Brian raised his glass of mineral water.

'Doctor's orders,' said Brian. 'No alcohol until I've lost 10 kilos, and there's no way I'm going home with booze on my breath. May will kill me.'

They laughed.

'So, does that mean you'll be ordering a salad?' said DI Williams, when he'd managed to regain control of himself.

'Afraid so.'

'It's all in a good cause, Brian. Just think of all that golf you'll be able to play when you retire to Victor,' said Stella, poking him in the ribs.

'I was hoping I'd be able to work on forever,' said Brian. 'Can't say I'm looking forward to living in one of those retirement villages May's got her heart set on.'

Over dinner their talk turned to other investigations and how Shaun was finding life in Adelaide after Melbourne.

By eight-thirty Shaun and Stella were sitting on their own.

'Must say I prefer watching you work in court to being interviewed by you,' said Stella. 'At least I don't have to worry about the cross examination when I'm just watching.'

'You did alright the last time I saw you being cross examined,' said Shaun. 'Not sure I'd like to be the person trying to undermine your evidence.'

'Yes, well let's hope we can finish this one with a better outcome than Genovese,' said Stella.

'Wasn't your fault that Roach reneged. At least someone's serving time for killing those girls.'

Shaun placed his hands over hers. 'So, what are you doing next?'

Stella smiled into his deep blue eyes. 'I was thinking of inviting you home to meet my family.'

A GUN OF MANY PARTS

STELLA BRUNO INVESTIGATES

A few Australian terms

Bikie is the Australian term for a biker or member of an outlaw motorcycle gang.

A **Stobie pole** is a power line pole made of two steel rails separated by a slab of concrete that is widely used throughout South Australia. See Wikipedia for more details and images.

Yatala is the name of the maximum security prison in Adelaide, South Australia.

CHAPTER 1

STELLA READ the incident report on the shooting written by the officers who had responded to the call. She thought it looked like this was going to be an open and shut case. They had listed the name of the perpetrator under the details of the victim. She suspected it would only be a matter of time before he was in custody.

Brian parked behind the patrol car outside the victim's house in Brunswick Street, Kilburn, a suburb still waiting for the arrival of the urban renewal movement transforming the city's public housing estates.

'Not my favourite suburb, Sarge,' said Brian, pressing the lock icon on the remote.

Stella looked up the street towards Prospect Road. 'There are worse places to live.'

They walked up to the tiny porch. Stella flashed her ID to the constable taking up most of the space outside the front door.

In the front room, immediately inside the door, a police-woman was sitting on a well-worn couch with a grey-haired woman clutching a box of tissues.

'I'm Detective Sergeant Bruno,' said Stella, 'and, this is Detective Constable Rhodes. We'd like to ask you a few questions, Mrs Barnes.'

The grey-haired woman looked up from her tissues.

'Were you here when it happened?' said Stella.

'Sitting right here, love. I told him not to get involved but he never listens to me, does he?'

'What didn't you want your husband to get involved in, Mrs Barnes?'

'That silly bitch next door was fighting with her boyfriend again. They were making such a racket we couldn't hear the telly. Jeff wanted to tell them to keep it down. I told him to leave it alone, it wouldn't go on for long. It never did. But he couldn't wait. Went out and told them to shut up.'

Stella waited. She didn't think Mrs Barnes would need much prompting now that she was off on her story.

'Next thing I know there's a bang and an almighty scream. I rushed out the front. Jeff was lying on the lawn. She was screaming her head off. The boyfriend got into his car and drove off.'

'Who called the ambulance?'

'She did. I didn't want to leave him.' Mrs Barnes stopped talking and wiped away her tears. 'I'm sorry, but he was all I had.'

'I'm sorry for your loss, Mrs Barnes,' said Stella.

Stella thought of her own loss every time she spoke to a person left behind after a senseless killing. She knew the pain of that loss never went away completely, no matter what you did. Stella didn't believe that time healed all hurts. She knew it only dulled the pain into something you could live with, but only if you didn't give it too much attention.

The door of the house next door was opened by a woman in her mid-thirties with bloodshot eyes. Stella wondered if she'd slept a wink since the shooting.

'Carol Jacobs?' said Stella.

The woman nodded. 'Who are you?'

'Detective Sergeant Bruno. I'd like to ask you a few questions.'

'Why? Didn't she tell you what happened?'

Stella wondered why she was so defensive.

'If you mean Mrs Barnes, she didn't see what happened, but I understand you did.'

'Yeah, well there's not much to tell, is there? Stupid bastard shot the old geezer, didn't he?'

'This would be Greg Allen?'

'Yeah. Wish I'd never met him. He's such a loser.'

'What was the fight about last night?'

Carol looked down at her bare feet. 'I told the prick to piss off. I was sick of him turning up half-tanked and expecting me to open my legs for him. Told him to piss off and not come back.'

'I take it he didn't go quietly,' said Stella.

Carol looked Stella in the eyes. 'Silly bastard pulled out a gun and waved it at me, threatened to blow my head off. That's when Mr Barnes came out and told us to shut the fuck up. Greg just turned and shot him. Then the idiot left.'

'Do you know where we can find him?'

'No. I don't know where he lives.'

On the drive back to the office, Stella and Brian listened to a radio call directing patrols to seal off an area surrounding Torrens Road, Kilkenny, where Allen's vehicle had been spotted.

'Let's hope he doesn't do anything stupid,' said Brian.

'Bit late for that, isn't it?' said Stella.

'You know what I mean. I hope he has the sense to turn himself in.'

'Who knows what he'll do, especially when he realizes he's cornered?

They listened to the radio chatter as the patrols coordinated their positions and the police helicopter arrived over the area.

'256. I see him. He's heading North on Torrens Road. I'm in pursuit.'

'Target vehicle turning left into Aroona Road,' said a voice from the police helicopter. 'Shit! He's lost it.'

Stella held her breath.

'He's hit the Stobie pole!' said the voice from the helicopter.

'Bloody hell!' said Brian. 'I hope he hasn't killed himself.'

They waited for the next update.

'No sign of the driver. 256 has arrived.'

They listened as the officer from patrol car 256 called for an ambulance and the fire service's jaws of life.

'Must have hit that Stobie pole pretty hard if they need the jaws of life,' said Stella.

'What was he driving again?' said Brian.

'A Toyota Corolla,' said Stella.

'Not enough steel in those things when you hit a Stobie pole at speed. He's probably wrapped it around the pole if he hit it side on.'

Stella thought about the impact. 'He was turning left, wasn't he?'

'Yeah. That's what he said.'

'He would have hit it on the driver's side,' said Stella. 'Don't like his chances.'

By the time they arrived back at the office, news had come through that Allen had been killed on impact when his vehicle slid across the intersection and collided with the Stobie pole on the corner of Aroona Road.

'This must be one of the shortest investigations we've been involved in, Sarge,' said Brian, as they waited in line to buy coffee.

'Let's hope they find his gun and match it with the bullet that killed Barnes,' said Stella. 'I'd hate to find out his girlfriend set him up, seeing she's the only witness to the shooting.'

'Hadn't thought of that.'

Stella didn't have to wait long to learn that the gun found in the wreckage of Allen's car had fired the shot that killed Jeff Barnes. The report from Ballistics was the first thing she read when she logged on the following morning.

As she studied the report, she realized it raised more questions than it answered.

'What are you reading?' said Brian, placing a coffee on her desk.

'Ballistics' report on the gun found in Allen's car.'

'What does it say?'

'He had a brand new Glock 19.'

'Did they match it with the round taken from the victim?'

'Yes.'

'So, case closed, then.' Brian took the lid off his coffee and sat down.

'I'm not so sure, Brian. We might have solved the murder but I think this opens another can of worms.'

'What do you mean?'

'Think about it. How did he get a Glock? They're on the prohibited list.'

'Maybe he managed to buy one on the internet. You know, a private sale from someone in the States. Anyone can buy a gun over there.' Brian sipped his coffee.

'I guess that's possible but it says here that the frame, barrel and slide have different serial numbers and, according to Ballistics, those numbers are the same on a new Glock when it's sold. And, this is a new Glock we're talking about.'

Brian scratched his head and took another sip of his coffee. 'Sounds like someone must have put it together from parts. Who would do that?'

'Somebody who has more than one of them, Brian.'

'So, maybe somebody is buying these things on the internet and selling them to idiots like Allen?'

'Maybe.' Stella leant back in her chair. 'See what we have on Allen. We'll need to find out who he was hanging around with. Think I'd better go speak with DI Williams.'

Stella drank her coffee, picked up the copy of the report she had printed, and headed for DI Williams' office.

The inspector was reading the morning paper when she knocked on his door.

'Got a minute, sir? Think we might have a problem.'

DI Williams looked up from his newspaper. 'What's on your mind, Bruno?'

'This report from Ballistics.'

'Is that on the gun from Allen's car?'

'Yes, and that's the problem. It's a Glock 19.'

'Aren't they prohibited?'

'They are,' said Stella.

'How the hell did he get one then?'

'Good question, sir. As a guess, I'd say someone is importing them as parts and putting them together for people like Allen.'

'What makes you think that?'

'Ballistics reckon Allen's Glock was put together using parts from at least three different weapons.'

'How did they work that out?'

'Different serial numbers on the main parts.'

'You'd think they'd erase the serial numbers, wouldn't you, Bruno? We must be dealing with amateurs,' said DI Williams.

'I gather that when Glock sells them the main parts have the same serial number. Certainly looks like our smuggler hasn't given much attention to the details.'

DI Williams closed his newspaper. 'If someone's managed to get three of these things into the country, I wonder how many more they've imported and where they are now.'

'Where do you think we should start?'

The inspector put out his hand for the report. 'See if you can find out where Allen got his Glock. That might lead us to whoever's smuggling these things into the country from this end. I'll see if we can find out who Glock sold the guns with these serial numbers to. That might help us track them from the other end.'

Brian was scrolling through pages on the database when Stella returned to her desk.

'Find anything?'

'Suspended driver's licence, twelve speeding fines, a couple of DUIs. Nothing to suggest he'd be running around with a gun.'

'Next of kin details?'

'Got his mother's address here. It's the same as the address on his driver's licence.'

'Guess we'd better go pay her a visit, and I'd like to interview his girlfriend again. She might be a bit more forthcoming now that he's no longer a threat.'

Forty minutes later, they were standing outside the house listed as the home of Teresa Allen in Andrews Road, Elizabeth Downs. The front lawn looked like it could use a cut and the garden beds were infested with weeds. There was a small red car parked in the driveway, so they assumed she was home.

Brian pushed the button for the doorbell. There no sound. He banged on the door.

'Hold your horses!'

A couple of minutes later, a small woman with jet black hair opened the door and glared at them.

'Who are you?'

Stella held out her ID. 'Detective Sergeant Bruno.'

'What do you want?'

Stella could smell the venom in her words.

'I'd like to talk to you about Greg.'

'Bit fucking late for that, isn't it?'

Stella thought she was going to shut the door on them.

'I know it's painful, Mrs Allen. I know what it's like to lose a loved one so unexpectedly, but you might be able to help me stop it happening to someone else.'

'How the fuck would you know what it's like?'

Stella looked her in the eye. 'My husband was killed by someone driving under the influence. Knocked him off his motorbike.' She paused and placed her hand over her heart. 'Believe me, Mrs Allen. I know how you feel.'

Mrs Allen looked at Stella and then at Brian. 'I suppose you'd better come in then.'

She led them into the front room where they sat on facing floral patterned couches. Stella glanced around and noticed the array of coloured-glass owls adorning every flat surface.

'What do you want to know?' said Mrs Allen.

'I'm trying to work out where Greg got the gun we found in his car. It's a prohibited import.'

'I didn't even know he had a gun until they came to tell me he was dead and that he'd shot that man.'

'I guess that must have come as a bit of a shock,' said Stella.

Mrs Allen shook her head. 'I knew he drank a bit and I didn't like some of his friends. But I never thought he'd shoot someone. It's not like he was some sort of gangster. Not like those idiots he was hanging out with.'

'Oh, who was he hanging out with?'

'Bikies! I told him not to have anything to do with them but he thought they were some sort of Robin Hood type heroes. You know, tough guys doing good deeds. Guess that's why he left home in the end. Didn't want to listen to me complaining about his mates.'

'Do you know the names of any of his mates?'

'No. They weren't the boys he went to school with. He met them at the pub and went out with them on weekends. I wouldn't let him bring them here with their bloody noisy motorbikes.'

'Which pub would that be?' said Stella.

'Some pub in Elizabeth. Don't know which one he went to. I only go to The Lodge.'

'Did Greg ride a motorbike?'

'That was another fight we had. Didn't stop him buying one though.'

'His driver's licence lists this address, so where was he living if he'd moved out?'

'He was sharing a house with a mate over in Paralowie. I've never been there.'

'Do you know this mate's name?'

'Doug something. Someone Greg met at work.'

'And, where was that?'

'Salisbury Council. He worked there as a gardener. Been there since he left school. At least that was one thing he did right.'

Half an hour after leaving Mrs Allen, they walked into the Municipal Offices of the City of Salisbury and asked to speak to someone in Human Resources.

After a short wait, the Human Resources Manager, a middle-aged man wearing a suit, came out to speak with them. 'How can I help you, Sergeant?'

Stella handed him a copy of Greg Allen's driver's licence. 'I'd like to confirm that this man worked here and talk to his work-mates. His mother told us he was a gardener here.'

'That's right, but he was terminated just over six months ago.'

Stella wondered why his mother didn't know that. 'Can you tell me why?' said Stella.

'Turned up drunk for work, despite several warnings. Shame really. He was a nice kid when he started.'

'His mother said he worked with someone called Doug. Any idea who that might be?'

'That would be Doug Watson.'

'I'd like to talk to him. Do you have his contact details?'

'Give me a minute. I'll find out where he is.'

Ten minutes later, they got out of the car and walked towards two men in dark blue and yellow clothing working in the park alongside the Little Para River.

The younger of the men stopped working and walked over to join them.

'You the police?'

Stella held out her ID. 'Detective Sergeant Bruno. This is Detective Constable Rhodes. I take it you're Doug Watson?'

'Yeah. Boss said you wanted to talk about Greg.'

'You're aware of the situation?'

'Yeah. Heard he was dead and that he's supposed to have shot some bloke.'

'You don't sound all that surprised.'

'I don't know what happened. He was a good bloke but then he started getting into fights at the pub and coming home pissed. I told him to get his act together but then he went and got himself sacked. I haven't seen him for six months.'

'Wasn't he living with you?' said Stella.

'Who told you that?'

'His mother.'

Doug smiled. 'He was for a while, but he's been living somewhere in the city since he lost his job here. I think he had a girlfriend down there some place.'

'Any idea who he was hanging around with after work?'

'Bunch of losers on motorbikes. You might find some of them drinking at the Salisbury.'

'Did you know he owned a gun?'

Doug shook his head. 'I never saw him with one, and he never talked about wanting one either. Just goes to show, doesn't it?'

'What do you mean?' said Stella.

'Thought I knew him. Obviously, I didn't.'

Carol Jacobs opened the door and invited them in when they knocked. Stella thought she looked as if she'd had a decent sleep since the last time they'd seen her.

'Thought you lot would be back.'

They sat around the table in Carol's small kitchen.

'Carol, we're trying to find out where Greg got his gun. Did you know he had one before the other night?' said Stella.

'I knew he had one. Reckoned he needed it for work.'

'What sort of work did he say he was doing?'

'Security.'

'Do you know where or which company he worked for?' said Stella.

Carol shook her head. 'Not really. He just said he was in security. I wasn't interested really. We weren't going anywhere.'

Stella wondered why women like Carol got themselves involved with men like Greg Allen. She couldn't imagine herself being in a casual relationship based solely on sex.

'When did you meet him?'

'About a year ago. Seemed like a nice guy at first, but then he started showing up pissed and wanting sex. I told him I didn't do sex with drunks.'

'Where did you meet him?'

'At HQ. I worked behind the bar before it closed. He was a regular.'

'Do you know where he was living?'

Carol shook her head. 'He always came here and I never asked. It's not like it was gonna last.'

'Did he talk about his friends with you?'

'The only thing he ever talked about with me was sex.' Carol leant back in her chair and laughed. 'He was sex mad.'

Stella looked at Carol and thought she could understand why a young man would be interested in her for sex. She was tall, had curves in all the right places and a disarming smile.

'Were you aware he was hanging around with some bikies out at Salisbury?'

'Bikies? Aren't they tough blokes with lots of tats?' Carol looked at Stella. 'Greg wasn't anything like that. He didn't even ride a motorbike as far as I know. He always came around in that red Toyota.'

After leaving Carol Jacobs, they headed back into the city.

'What do you think, Brian?'

'There was nothing about him having a security licence in the database, so whatever security work he was doing it had to be some private arrangement.'

'Seems to me those bikies must be the missing link.' Stella gazed out the window at the passing suburb. 'I wonder how we're going to find out where he was living.'

'I wonder if he was on the dole,' said Brian. 'Six months is a long time without a pay cheque coming in.'

'That gets paid into your bank account,' said Stella.

'Yeah, but he might have given Centrelink his current address given that he would have to report in regularly.'

'Give them a call. You might strike it lucky. I think I need to speak to someone on the Bikie Taskforce.'

Stella took out her mobile phone and scrolled through her contacts and then pressed the call button.

'Hi, Tim. Stella.'

'Hello, gorgeous. What can I do for you?'

Stella smiled. Tim Wilde, who had been Rick's best man at their wedding, was the only member of the force that flirted with her.

'You don't by any chance know which bikies would be hanging out at the Salisbury pub, do you?'

'They'd be Mongrels, Stella. That's their territory. Why do you want to know that?'

'I'm trying to find out where my killer got his gun.'

'What sort of gun?'

'A Glock 19, and a new one at that.'

'What's the name of your killer?'

'Allen. Greg Allen.'

'Give me a minute.'

Stella could hear the sound of keyboard clicks.

'He's not a member, but we've got him listed as someone to watch.'

'You wouldn't have an address, would you?'

'We have a place in Paralowie.'

'I've spoken to the guy that lives there. Told me Allen had moved out six months ago. I guess it wouldn't be a good idea for me to speak to any of these Mongrels, would it, Tim?'

'Leave that to me. I'll get back to you if we find out anything. I take it this Allen guy is the one that wiped himself out the other day.'

'That's him. You might want to update your spreadsheet, Tim, and thanks.'

CHAPTER 2

'I'LL CATCH YOU TOMORROW, SARGE.'

Stella looked up and waved as Brian headed towards the lifts and then sat staring at the screen of her computer. It was blank. She had already logged off for the day but she wasn't quite ready to leave. She was thinking about Shaun and what he'd asked her over lunch.

He'd asked her to spend the weekend with him at Victor. Just the two of them. No kids. He wanted to move on to the next phase in their relationship, beyond kissing and holding hands. She'd said she'd let him know once she'd made arrangements for Josh. He'd said he'd need to confirm the booking by Wednesday.

Over lunch she'd wanted to go. Now, she was having second thoughts and wondering whether she was ready to commit to having sex with Shaun. She knew she liked him, perhaps loved him, but she hadn't shared her bed or her body with a man since Rick and she was feeling a little nervous about doing it again.

She assumed the sex would happen naturally if it was meant to happen. It wasn't like she'd need to practice. She smiled as she thought of the first time she'd made love to Rick. That had been on a weekend away from home, too. But not a planned weekend like Shaun had in mind. It had happened one night when they'd been in Mt Gambier as part of a team monitoring a bikie gathering. That was the weekend she'd realized she loved Rick, and it hadn't been long after that she'd agreed to marry him.

She wondered why she hadn't just said yes to Shaun because getting someone to look after Josh for the weekend was a non-issue. Her parents or her brother and his wife did it without her even having to ask whenever she was rostered on over a weekend. She knew her sister-in-law, Denise, would volunteer as soon as she told her what Shaun had in mind. She could even picture the look that would light up Denise's face when she told her.

Stella took out her mobile phone and scrolled through her photos of Rick. He looked so young. He'd only been thirty-two when she'd lost him. He would have been forty-one next birthday. She wondered if he'd have gone bald like his father, who'd lost most of his hair by the time he was forty.

'What do you think, Rick? Am I doing the right thing? What would you do if it was you in my place?'

She knew the answer to that last question. Rick would have been remarried by now. He'd never liked being on his own. She was the one that had refused to let him go and even consider another man until Shaun had come along.

She picked up her handbag and walked over to the lifts and pressed the button for the ground floor. When she arrived in the lobby, she walked out into the street and made her way to Rundle Mall where the shops were, and spent the next hour buying herself new underwear.

When she got back to her car, she called Shaun. Her call went through to voice mail before she remembered he'd be at the gym.

'Shaun, It's Stella. Count me in for the weekend. Give me a call when you get this. Love you.'

Those two little words she'd uttered at the end without

thinking reverberated in her mind. She'd told him she loved him. She'd never said that to any man except Rick before.

'I hope you know what you're doing, Stella.'

She inserted the key into the ignition and started the engine.

'Feels right to me!'

***

On Wednesday morning, Centrelink confirmed Greg Allen had been receiving the Newstart Allowance and provided Stella with an address in Ena Street, Croydon Park.

'Guess now we know why he was in Kilkenny,' said Brian, when Stella told him the news.

'Let's go and see if anybody's home,' said Stella.

Twenty minutes later they were standing on the front veranda of a red brick house with an overgrown front lawn.

'Guess he didn't bring any of his gardening skills with him,' said Brian, as they waited to see if there was anyone home.

They were just about to leave when the front door opened.

'Yeah?' said a man, rubbing sleep from his eyes.

Stella held out her ID. 'Police.'

'Who are you looking for?'

'Do you know Greg Allen?' said Stella.

The man looked at Stella and then at Brian.

'Haven't seen him since last week. What's he done this time?'

Stella looked at Brian.

'What's your connection to Greg?' said Stella.

'I'm just a mate. He needed somewhere to live when he lost his job. I needed someone to look after the place when I'm not here. I work at Prominent Hill. You know, one week on, one week off. I only got home last night.'

'Mind telling me your name, sir?' said Stella.

'Jack, Jack Richards.'

'Jack, Greg's dead. He was killed when his car hit a Stobie pole last Friday.'

'If you know that, why are you here?'

'We've only just found out this was where he was living.'

'Oh. Have you told his Mum?'

'Yes, we've spoken with his mother,' said Stella. 'Were you aware Greg owned a pistol, Jack?'

Jack shook his head. 'I knew he had some shady mates but I didn't know he had a gun.'

'He used it to shoot an elderly man on Thursday night.'

'Was that the shooting at Kilburn that was on the news?' said Jack.

'Yes,' said Stella. 'Did he leave any stuff here?'

'Yeah. His gear's still in his room.'

'Do you mind if we have a look?'

'Don't you need a search warrant or something to do that?'

'Not if you let us in, Jack.'

Jack stood still for several moments and then invited them in. 'That's the room he was using.' He pointed to the doorway immediately to the right as they entered the corridor that ran down the centre of the house. 'I'll be in the kitchen if you need me, down the end there.'

Stella surveyed the bedroom Greg Allen had used. The bed was unmade, as if he'd just got up and left the house. There was a built-in wardrobe along one wall with a set of drawers and hanging space for clothes.

'Doesn't look like our man had many clothes,' said Brian, when he opened the sliding door of the hanging space.

Stella looked under the bed while Brian opened the drawers.

'Got a box of ammo and a cleaning kit here, Sarge.'

'Bag that and anything else you find, Brian. Think I'll go have a chat with Jack.'

Stella went down the corridor to the kitchen where Jack was drinking a cup of tea.

'Where did you meet Greg?' said Stella.

'I worked with him at Salisbury before I got the job at Prominent Hill.'

'What do you do up there?'

'Security.'

'Ever try to get Greg a job there?'

'I offered to see if I could get him something but he wasn't interested.' Jack shook his head. 'It's too far away for a lot of these young blokes. They can't bear being away from their girlfriends.'

'You don't, by any chance, know if he had a motorbike?'

'He sold it and bought that red car of his a couple of years ago, when he stopped hanging around with his bikie mates.'

'Any idea who he was hanging around with over the last few months?'

'Me, when I was here. Got no idea what he was doing when I wasn't here, except that he was always talking about some tart called Carol he'd taken a fancy to.'

'Yes, I've met her. It was her next door neighbour he shot.' Stella paused. 'He wasn't into drugs, was he?'

'Smoked a bit of grass but the booze was his problem. Silly bugger lost his licence last time you lot pulled him over. Didn't stop him driving, though.'

'Pity,' said Stella. 'He might still be alive if it had.'

***

Stella went to see DI Williams when they got back to the office from Croydon Park.

'We've found out where he was living, but no-one seems to know what he was doing with his time apart from drinking and abusing his girlfriend, and she's the only one that knew he had a gun.'

'What's her story?'

'Claims Allen told her he worked in security but no-one in the industry has heard of him and he didn't have a licence. The bloke whose house he was looking after works in security at Prominent Hill. So, I think he might have spun her a yarn.'

'Find anything out from Tim Wilde?'

'Said Allen was on their watch list as someone hanging around with known members of the Mongrels but no-one's saying anything. Wilde's contacts are saying he was a hanger on full of piss.'

The inspector leant back in his chair. Stella thought she could see a smile in his eyes and wondered what he'd found out from his enquiries.

'Think we might keep the Mongrels in mind, Bruno. They're his most likely source no matter what Wilde's informants are telling him.' The smile made it to his face. 'There have been some interesting developments my end while you've been running around after Allen.'

'Oh, what did you find out from Austria?'

'Glock gave them the name of a gun dealer in Munich. Apparently, they sold the guns that go with our three serial numbers to him in July last year.'

The smile was now spreading across the inspector's face, so Stella knew he had more good news to share.

'I've been in contact with Munich. They've got our man under surveillance.'

'So, now we wait?'

'If they're still importing from this dealer, we only have to wait until he sends their next order.'

'How will Munich know?'

'They're watching his mailings. These clowns might be able

to order over the internet but he still has to post the guns to them, doesn't he?'

By the time they had negotiated their way through the Friday night rush hour traffic heading south and reached Darlington, they had been on the road for nearly an hour. The going got easier when they entered the Southern Expressway, where the traffic moved at the 100 kph speed limit, but it still took them another forty minutes to reach Victor Harbor.

Shaun parked the car in front of the Hotel Victor and went inside to check in. With the formalities over, he moved the car into the car park behind the hotel and they made their way upstairs to their room.

The room had a queen-size double bed and a view across the lawns of Warland Reserve to the ocean. Not that they had come to Victor to enjoy the view.

They dumped their overnight bags on the floor. Stella sat on the bed. It felt comfortable enough.

They made use of the facilities and then went downstairs to the restaurant.

'Shall we try the buffet, tonight? We can see what the a` la carte menu is like tomorrow night,' said Shaun.

'There are other places to eat down here, you know. Why don't we splash out on the a` la carte and find somewhere else for tomorrow?'

Shaun picked up the menu. 'Sounds like a plan.'

'Besides, Shaun, there's no need to rush. I'm not going anywhere.' Stella smiled.

She thought he looked as apprehensive as she felt. She hadn't been naked with a man for nine years. She wondered if she'd be able to relax enough so they would both enjoy the experience.

She reached across the table and touched his face. 'It'll be fine, Shaun.'

He smiled. 'Want a drink?'

'I'll have a glass of Chardonnay.'

'Why don't we get a bottle?'

They spent two hours in the restaurant talking, watching other people and enjoying their meal.

'Shall we go for a walk?' said Stella. 'It looks like a nice night out there.'

'I need a pee first,' said Shaun.

'Sounds like a good idea. I'll meet you out the front.'

They walked across the jetty that connected the mainland to Granite Island and kissed in the dark. Then they walked back to the hotel and made their way to their room.

Stella pulled the covers back on the bed and undressed, dropping her new underwear on top of her discarded clothes on the chair next to the bed. Shaun watched her and then took off his clothes.

'I'd forgotten how big those things were,' said Stella, wrapping her arms around him and pressing her breasts into his chest.

Shaun kissed her and gently lowered her onto the bed.

Stella relaxed into their love making, and when it was over, wondered what on earth she had been worried about.

'Can we do that again?'

There was no reply. Shaun was already asleep and snoring softly beside her on the bed.

She nudged him in the side. 'Did you hear me? I want more.'

He opened an eye and winked at her. 'I heard you, but I need to recharge my battery before I can do that again.'

She hit him with a pillow.

By the time they were checking out on Sunday morning, Stella knew she wanted more of Shaun and wondered why she'd waited so long to let another man into her life.

'Did you enjoy that?' said Shaun, as they climbed into the car. 'When can we do it again?'

'What part do you mean? Come to Victor or make love?'

'The make love part. We don't have to come all the way down here to do that. I have a perfectly good bed at home.'

'Yes, I've got one too but there are the kids to consider.'

'Oh, I'm sure Sarah's old enough to understand how it works and Josh is already asking me when you're coming over to sleep?'

Shaun looked at her as he turned the key in the ignition. 'I'm glad we took the risk.'

'Me, too.'

CHAPTER 3

THREE WEEKS after starting their surveillance operation, the police in Munich advised DI Williams that the gun dealer they were watching had mailed a package, addressed to a Mr A Einstone, PO Box 304 Brompton SA 5007, Australia, through Deutsche Post, and that the documentation submitted to clear Customs described its contents as technical drawing pens.

DI Williams established a communications channel with Australian Border Force, advised them of the impending arrival of the package, and discussed coordinating a sting to capture the perpetrators if the contents were what he thought they were.

Stella was tasked with identifying the intended recipient before the anticipated arrival of the package in three weeks time.

As soon as she had the details, Stella queried White Pages online and the Electoral Roll for anyone with that surname living in the area serviced by the Brompton Post Office.

'Think we might have an invented name, Brian. What do you think?'

'Sounds like one to me. These blokes might think they're smart but they're not that clever, are they? Albert Einstein. I ask you?'

'Someone must be paying for that PO Box. Perhaps we only have to ask Australia Post.'

'He could have used false ID. Not that hard to make these days. Remember that bloke who impersonated Bob Cunningham? Besides, it might not be a real post office.'

'What do you mean? Aren't they all real post offices?'

'They're not all run by Australia Post these days. It could be a licensed shop.'

'What's the difference?'

'If it's licensed, it's basically a shop that sells postal services and other stuff.'

Stella thought about all the merchandise on display at her local post office and wondered if it was one of these licensed shops. She'd always thought of it as the post office, since it had a large red and white Australia Post sign on its front window.

'How can we find out?'

'Let me do a search on Australia Post.' Brian opened the Australia Post website, keyed the postcode for Brompton into the location search field, and clicked on search. 'It's an LPO. A licensed post office on Torrens Road, not far from where Allen was living.'

'Guess we'd better talk to Australia Post and find out who the licensee is then.'

'That might not help, Sarge. Apparently, a lot of businesses take on more than one post office and put managers in to run their stores.'

'Where do you get this information, Brian?'

'Martha works in one of these places.'

'I thought she was working for an optometrist.'

'He got old and sold up. The new bloke didn't want her. Had his own girl. She's only just got a new job at her local post office. It's one of these licensed shops.' Brian smiled. 'They were over last weekend and I got the low down on how it all works.'

Stella imagined the scene. She'd met Martha and seen her in action. Martha had taken after her mother when it came to telling you anything. She felt sorry for Brian but he seemed to manage being harassed by the women in his life without too much stress.

Stella arranged the appropriate warrant and contacted Australia Post. They asked her to email through her request with a copy of the warrant attached.

By the end of the day, they knew the post office at Brompton was one of three that Australia Post had licensed to JP Withers Pty Ltd, a private company with three shareholders all named Withers. Australia Post's response to Stella's request also advised that the company had held the licence for the Brompton Post Office for the last three years and that there had been no customer complaints about their service.

Brian's check of the Withers named by Australia Post on the database turned up a nil result for all three.

'We don't know anything about these people,' said Brian. 'At least, they've never committed a serious crime.'

'That doesn't mean they're innocent parties, Brian. It just means they haven't come to our attention before.'

Stella considered her options.

'You know, it's possible someone is using that post office box to avoid the parcel being delivered to a residential address. Anybody can hire a post office box. We might be able to set up a camera to find out who is using that box.' She looked at Brian. 'But what if it's the person running the post office? It would be the perfect set up, wouldn't it? He could use any name as long as he had the guns delivered to Brompton, and they'd never be collected by someone with the key to box 304.'

'Think you might be on to something there, Sarge.'

Stella realized she couldn't risk speaking to the Withers in case they were behind the scheme to import the guns.

'We need to find out who's working in that shop, Brian. I think first thing tomorrow we might go and buy some stamps.'

It was five to ten on a Wednesday morning, when Brian turned off Torrens Road into the tiny car park of the small Brompton Shopping Centre and parked the car in one of the three vacant parking spaces in front of the Foodworks Supermarket.

'Busy little place,' said Stella, as they climbed out of the car.

The post office was a single fronted shop next to the supermarket. They walked past the colourful front windows of the supermarket advertising the week's specials and into the small post office. Brian stood just inside the door with his iPhone in his hand and examined the merchandise on display. Stella took off her sunglasses and approached the young man behind the counter at the rear of the space. She noted the tattoo on his neck and guessed he was in his thirties.

'How can I help you?'

'Book of ten stamps, please.'

The man opened a drawer in the counter and took out a book of stamps.

'Anything else?'

'No, that's all I need,' said Stella, handing him a twenty dollar note.

She watched to see where he touched the book of stamps as he slid it across the counter to her, and folded the ten dollar note he gave her as change around the stamps before putting them into her purse.

'Thank you.' She turned and headed towards the door.

Brian raised his iPhone and took her photograph as she walked towards him.

'Will you cut that out!' said Stella. 'Haven't you got enough photos of me by now?'

'Sorry, honey, but you look so gorgeous in this light.'

Stella thumped him in the shoulder as she walked past him and out the door.

Brian shrugged his shoulders at the man standing behind the counter, who was laughing at their antics.

'Women. Who understands them?' said Brian, slipping his iPhone into his pocket and following Stella out to the car.

'Probably a one man operation,' said Stella, when Brian closed the door.

'He's standing in the shop doorway,' said Brian.

'Let's go then.'

Brian started the car and backed out of the parking space. He waited for the lady in the small green car that had backed out from a parking bay in front of the post office to move off, and waved to the man from the post office as they drove past him on their way out of the car park.

'Did you get him?' said Stella.

Brian handed her his iPhone and she looked at the photograph he had taken inside the post office.

'Nice shot, Brian.'

'It's all that practice I get snapping you, honey.'

Stella laughed. 'You're a real card sometimes, Brian.'

'I do my best.'

Twenty minutes later, Stella handed her book of stamps into Forensics and asked them to see if the finger prints on the front cover belonged to anyone they knew. The officer slipped the cover under a light on his desk.

'There's a good clear print there. I'll make a copy and run it through the database for you, Sarge. I'll let you know if I get a hit.'

Stella was having coffee with Brian in the shop at street level when her mobile phone rang.

'DS Bruno.'

'I've got something for you, Sergeant. Your finger print belongs to someone we know.'

'Send me the details, and thanks, John.' She looked at Brian. 'That was Forensics. They got a match.'

The details were waiting in Stella's inbox when she got back to her desk. The finger print she had obtained from the man in the post office belonged to Andrew Knight, a member of the Mongrels who had served a short prison term for assault. He had been back on the streets for five years and had not reoffended in that time.

She called Tim Wilde.

'Tim, what can you tell me about a Mongrel called Andrew Knight?'

'Andrew Knight? He's been pretty quiet since his stay in Yatala. Why do you want to know?'

'He's working at the Brompton Post Office, and that's where my parcel of guns is headed.'

'We need to talk.'

'DI Williams' Office would be a good place. I'm heading there now.'

Sergeant Tim Wilde listened as Stella told DI Williams about Andrew Knight managing the Brompton Post Office.

'What do you know about this Knight fellow, Wilde?' said DI Williams.

Stella noticed he spoke to Tim the same way he spoke to her and wondered whether he spoke to all sergeants that way, and not just her.

'Don't think he's smart enough to be doing this on his own,

Inspector. He was working as a barista in a place owned by one of his mates before we sent him to prison.'

'How does someone with his background get to be running a post office?' said DI Williams.

'We need to find out more about these Withers people,' said Stella. 'Maybe they're the ones behind this operation and Knight is just their front man.'

'Knight's the only one known to us,' said Tim. 'As far as I know, there is no-one called Withers associated with the Mongrels.'

'That doesn't mean they aren't doing business with them though, does it?' said DI Williams.

'That would definitely have to be clandestine, Inspector. There's not much we don't know about the Mongrels,' said Tim.

'It's always the stuff we don't know that bites us in the bum, Sergeant.'

The inspector paced back and forth in front of his desk and then sat on the edge of the desk.

'OK. I want a wire on the telephone in that shop and on any numbers linked to Knight. Wilde, your taskforce has the resources to do that. Get it set up and pass the transcripts to Bruno.'

'Yes, sir.'

'Bruno, I want you to find out as much as you can on these Withers people. We need to know if they're involved or being taken advantage of, and we need to find out who's financing this operation.'

'If they've been at it for a while, there must be someone in on it that understands how to do the paperwork on imports to get their guns through Customs,' said Tim, 'otherwise, you'd think they would have been picked up by now.'

'I gather there's so much stuff coming in from all this online shopping we're doing that Customs can't check it all. They told me they have to run some sort of risk assessed system, otherwise they'd have a mountain of packages to go through and they're not resourced to do that' said DI Williams. 'At least they'll inspect this package. They're waiting for it.'

'Of course, there could be someone in Customs making sure their stuff gets through,' said Stella.

'Border Force are looking into that possibility,' said DI Williams, 'but their people are vetted before they get employed and closely monitored, so I wouldn't invest too much in that theory, Bruno. Besides, that's their problem. We need to focus on getting our end sorted.'

'Perhaps we could ask Munich to trace the money trail. That gun dealer must get paid somehow,' said Stella.

'They're looking in to that,' said DI Williams. 'I'll let you know what they come up with.'

Armed with the information on JP Withers Pty Ltd provided by Australia Post, Stella searched the Australian Business Register and the companies register maintained by the Australian Securities and Investment Commission.

Her searches revealed that JP Withers Pty Ltd owned three news agencies in addition to the three licensed post offices it operated on behalf of Australia Post, and that the company had been in business for thirty-six years. At least, it had been registered for that length of time, which meant the same thing to Stella.

From the records in the public domain, she discovered that the James Patrick Withers, after whom the company was named, was in his eighties, and that the William and Henry Withers named as shareholders in the privately held company were James' sons.

'This doesn't look like a crime family to me, Brian.'

'What does a crime family look like, Sarge?'

'I mean, it all looks legitimate on paper. Besides, you'd think we'd know something about them if they were operating on the wrong side of the law. They've been in business for nearly forty years.'

'Things change, Sarge. The news agency business isn't what it used to be when I started on the job. Everybody was reading a paper on the train in those days. Now they've all got their noses stuck in some electronic device.' Brian smiled. 'And when was the last time you sent someone a card or bought a magazine?'

'Guess that's why they've moved into Post Offices.'

'Another failing business.'

'Australia Post?'

'They're not making any money from delivering letters. Seen all that stuff they have for sale in a post office? If it wasn't for all those parcels they deliver from our online shopping they'd be broke.' Brian shook his head. 'Once, all they did was deliver the mail, sell money orders, and send telegrams. You do know what a telegram is, don't you?'

'Only from the movies. I've never actually seen one,' said Stella.

'And, you're not likely to see one either. It's all email or text messages now. Even May's into texting. A bloke can't even escape when he's down the pub!'

Stella smiled. 'You could turn your phone off, you know, Brian.'

'Yeah, like that would be a good idea.'

Stella laughed.

'So, you think these guys might have been tempted into smuggling guns to make ends meet?'

'They wouldn't be the first people to do something stupid to avoid bankruptcy.'

'They'd have to be desperate though, wouldn't they? That's a big line to cross. Surely, they'd be selling assets if they were in trouble, not taking on extra licensed post offices, don't you think? And, you'd think Australia Post would do some due diligence on the people they sign on.'

'Let's see if they've sold anything in the last year or so,' said Brian.

'You do that, and perhaps after lunch we could drive by their shops and see what they look like.'

While Brian spoke to their contact at the State Revenue Office, which tracked land and vehicle sales, Stella looked up the locations of the three news agencies the company operated. One was at Westfield Marion, another was at Westfield West Lakes, and the third was at Westfield Tea Tree Plaza.

'I'm not so sure these guys would be in financial difficulty, Brian. Their shops are all in Westfield Shopping Centres, so they must be making enough money to pay the rent, and I hear rent in those shopping centres is at the high end of the market.'

'And, they haven't sold off any assets either. In fact, Henry has bought two properties, and they don't look cheap going by what you can see on Google Maps.'

'I wonder how Knight got the job at Brompton. How old is he?' said Stella.

Brian reviewed the print he'd made of Knight's listing in the database. 'Thirty-five.'

'I wonder if William and Henry have any sons of their own. Maybe Knight is a friend of a friend or a mate.'

'It says here Knight went to Prince Alfred's. Looks like he's one of those kids from a rich family that's taken a wrong turn.'

'He could have some interesting connections with money then, couldn't he?'

'Maybe we're dealing with some smart-arse yuppies taking the piss out of the Mongrels and not someone fronting for them,' said Brian. 'Be interesting to see who turns up on those phone taps.'

Before any results came through from the wire on Knight's phone, Stella received a call from Ballistics.

'Sergeant, we've got another Glock. A new 19 with mismatched serial numbers like the one we tested for you.'

'Where did it come from?' said Stella.

'From the kid that held up the Caltex servo on Salisbury Highway last night.'

'Whose case is it?'

'It came from Sergeant Murray, out at Elizabeth.'

Stella looked up his number.

'Simon, Stella Bruno. Understand you arrested a young man who held up a service station with a pistol.'

'Gee, news travels fast, Stella.'

'I'm particularly interested in Glocks at the moment, Simon. I'm trying to identify who's smuggling them into the country and who's buying them. What's this kid saying about where he got the pistol?'

'Claims he borrowed it, without asking, of course. It wasn't loaded.'

'What's the kid's name?'

'Watson. Chris Watson.'

That name sounded familiar to Stella. 'Who does he claim he borrowed it from?'

'He's not saying.'

'How old is this kid?'

'He's not really a kid, Stella. He's nineteen. Old enough to know better.'

'Does he happen to have a brother called Doug?'

'How did you know that?'

'I had occasion to speak to a Doug Watson in relation to someone else with a Glock who had shared a house with him. Lives in Paralowie and works for the Salisbury Council.'

'Not sure if they're related. This boy's brother works at Roxby. He's up there this week but he's also a member of the Mongrels. I wouldn't be surprised if the gun belongs to him and, if that's the case, he's not likely to claim it or tell us where he got it.'

'Don't think I'd like to be in the boy's shoes when his brother gets home, if that's the case.'

'He's consumed too much ice to be worried about the consequences of his actions. We're probably lucky he couldn't find any ammo. He was off his face when we picked him up.'

'Let me know if he changes his tune about where the gun came from. For the time being, I'll pass on what you've told me about the brother but I'll leave any follow up to you. We don't want to alert anyone that we're on to these weapons being smuggled in at the moment.'

When she'd finished speaking with Simon Murray, Stella called Tim Wilde.

'Tim, we've got another Glock in the system. Taken from a kid that tried to hold up a service station last night. I've just been on the phone to Simon Murray at Elizabeth. The kid's brother is a member of the Mongrels.'

'What's his name?'

'Doug Watson.'

'Yeah, not someone you'd want to meet on a dark night, Stella,' said Tim. 'He works for security at Roxby. Used to be in the army.'

'It's possible the Glock's his. Apparently, the kid claims he borrowed it. Simon says he's an ice addict and was off his face when they picked him up.'

'Don't think I'd like to be him when his big brother finds out, if the gun's his,' said Tim.

Stella ended the call and thought about the Glocks. She wondered how many of them were in circulation.

She called Ballistics.

'Do any of the serial numbers on the Glock that came in this morning match the numbers on Allen's Glock?'

'No, Sergeant. They're all different. I'd say you have at least another four to find.'

'How much do these things cost?'

'In a place where you can buy them legally, around five hundred US dollars. Guess they'd be a bit more than that on the black market.'

Stella wondered how much money was behind the operation. She knew the Mongrels were suspected of being behind the latest ice epidemic and supposed they could be cashed up. If it was their operation, she feared there could be hundreds of guns on the street.

That was a thought she didn't want to contemplate. She hoped it was a small-time operation, with Knight acting alone or with one or two others. That way, there might only be tens of guns, unless Knight had a financial backer with deep pockets.

No matter how she thought about it, she didn't like the scenario that came to mind.

CHAPTER 4

THE LOCATION of the Brompton Post Office, in a small shopping centre across the road from the grounds of the Brompton Primary School, created a problem for Tim Wilde. Any surveillance unit he set up in the shopping centre's car park or across the road in front of the schoolyard would be obvious to anyone who noticed his surroundings.

After considering the options proposed by his team, Sergeant Wilde had a group of officers dressed as SA Power Network employees install a camera on the Stobie pole in front of the shopping centre and streamed its recordings to the surveillance team sitting in a van parked around the corner in Wattle Street.

A second team watched Knight's residence in nearby Coglin Street from cars that were parked in front of different houses each night.

The listening into Knight's telephone conversations took place inside Police Headquarters, where a team of officers rotated through the headsets to continuously monitor what was said on the telephone in the post office and on his private mobile number. In addition to the monitoring, the conversations were recorded to create the evidence trail required for a conviction.

The first week of listening revealed nothing of value, apart from identifying Knight's current girlfriend and establishing that he reported to Henry Withers at the end of each day before shutting the shop.

Stella ran background checks on Julia Mahoney and discovered she was a teacher at Brompton Primary School and the sister of one of Knight's school friends, a lawyer who often represented members of outlawed motorcycle gangs in court. The surveillance team in Coglin Street confirmed she was living in the house with Knight.

Early in the second week of listening, Knight received a call on his mobile from a male asking if the pens had arrived from Germany. Knight told him he was still waiting for the package and would let him know when it arrived. The caller had then asked when he'd be placing the next order, as he thought they'd have more customers than the number of pens they had in the pipeline. Knight had replied he'd check with Einstone and get back to him.

When the male caller was identified as Mark Roberts, the owner of a motorcycle repair shop in Salisbury, Tim Wilde informed DI Williams that Roberts was a senior figure within the Mongrels and requested permission to increase the scope of their surveillance to listening in on his communications.

Twenty-four hours later, with the authorizations in place, the Bikie Taskforce expanded the scope of their surveillance to Roberts. Over the next few days, the listeners picked up several calls to Robert's mobile number from men wanting to know when they'd be getting their new pens.

Stella's research on the mobile phone numbers revealed the calls Roberts was receiving were coming from people listed in Tim Wilde's spreadsheet of known Mongrels.

Late on the Friday afternoon of the second week of their surveillance, DI Williams called Stella and Tim into a briefing.

'Border Force has advised the package is in Sydney,' said DI Williams.

'What's in it?' said Stella.

'Twenty-five Glock slides and magazines, and twenty boxes of technical drawing pens,' said DI Williams.

'So, they're importing them in parts as we suspected,' said Stella.

'Everybody seems to know these guns are on their way,' said Tim. 'They're all getting impatient, so I guess these must be the final parts for putting together twenty-five Glocks.'

'You'd think they were part of a drawing club, not a motor-cycle club, going on these transcripts,' said DI Williams, dropping the papers he was holding onto his desk.

'At least we know where the guns appear to be going, sir,' said Stella.

'How many members does this club have?' said DI Williams.

'Around twenty locally but close to a hundred across the eastern states,' said Tim.

'We're going to need people when we're ready to move,' said DI Williams, 'if we're going to have any hope of getting these weapons out of circulation before they realize we're on to them.'

'Do we know when the package will be delivered?' said Stella.

'Wednesday, and I don't want anything going wrong on the day. I want the logistics for the raids finalized over the weekend. We'll hit the post office and the bike repair shop, and Knight's and Roberts' homes on Wednesday if it becomes clear no-one else is involved, and every other member of the gang early Thursday morning. I want a detailed plan on my desk first thing Monday morning.'

Stella looked at Tim and hoped they'd be able to work it out on Saturday as she had other plans for Sunday, the first day she'd be having off since the investigation had started.

'I've got most of that worked out already, sir,' said Tim. 'I'll go through it with Stella tomorrow to make sure we have everything covered, so Monday shouldn't be a problem.'

Stella wanted to hug him but remember where she was and smiled instead.

When the meeting ended, Stella went back to her desk and briefed Brian.

'Hope we get this sorted tomorrow, Sarge. I've got plans for Sunday that don't involve coming in here.'

'Me, too, Brian.'

***

The Bikie Taskforce had contingency plans drawn up for raiding every known bikie gang in the state.

Stella and Tim spent Saturday conducting a thorough review of the plans Tim had drawn up based on his contingency plan for the Mongrels.

They decided they had sufficient officers within the Bikie Taskforce to conduct the raids on the post office, the motorcycle repair shop and the homes of Knight and Roberts on Wednesday, and drew up team lists for each location.

Most of their day was spent negotiating with Operations for the required number of officers and vehicles to conduct simultaneous raids on the thirty homes and businesses associated with the gang's members in the early hours of Thursday morning.

When they had the list of available officers, they assigned four officers to each address and compiled a list of officers who could be called into action at short notice to fill in if required.

Then, they prepared the briefing notes to be given to the officer in charge of each raid, detailing their objective, the need for coordination, and reminding them they were dealing with armed and dangerous bikies likely to resist arrest and not cooperate in any search. Finally, they drafted the communication DI

Williams would send to each officer selected to participate in the raids.

Brian spent the day preparing the mountain of paperwork DI Williams would need to get authorization to conduct the raids and search the identified premises for guns.

———

Shaun and Sarah arrived at ten thirty on Sunday morning to pick up Stella for their trip to Clare.

'You sit in the front with Dad, Stella. I've got a lecture to catch up on and a shitload of reading to do,' said Sarah.

She gave Stella a hug and slipped into the back seat of the car where she plugged her headphones into her laptop.

Stella slipped in beside Shaun. They exchanged a quick kiss and she buckled up.

'How's Josh?' said Shaun, as they exited the driveway.

'He's at soccer. You should come out and watch him play. Stefano reckons he's good.'

'Hope he isn't upset that I'm taking you away from seeing him play this week.'

'It's not my recognition he's after.' Stella laughed. 'I'm not the one who played for Adelaide City. That was Stefano, but I'm sure he'd get a buzz out of you coming to a game.'

'Not that I know anything about the round ball game. It was all Aussie Rules when I was growing up,' said Shaun.

'Doubt that would matter. It's you being there that would count.'

'Okay. Give me the details. I should be able to go next Sunday. Perhaps we can go together. Will you be off work?'

'Should be, unless something ugly happens.'

Shaun gave his attention to the traffic as he turned onto Grand Junction Road.

'How's that case of yours going?'

'We're getting to the pointy end. Our package is due to arrive on Wednesday,' said Stella.

'And, does it contain what you thought it would?'

'Would you believe it's actually got drawing pens in it along with the other stuff?'

'You're kidding. Isn't that what they were talking about between themselves?'

'They aren't the first people to smuggle stuff in with legitimate goods, Shaun. Happens all the time.'

'Guess they think they were being clever talking about the pens in case someone was listening in.'

'Everybody watches too much TV these days, if you ask me. If they were really clever, they'd know if we're listening we're on to them.'

'The criminal mind never ceases to amaze me, Stella. I'm looking forward to this case.'

Shaun parked the car in the driveway of his parents' house in William Street.

'Lovely garden,' said Stella, as she climbed out of the car into the sunshine.

'Mum's a keen gardener. That's another reason she refused to leave this house when Dad retired,' said Shaun, opening the boot and picking up the little esky he used for transporting wine bottles.

They walked around to the back of the house where an older version of Shaun, wearing a black apron, was fiddling with a large gas fired barbecue.

'How are you, Dad?' said Shaun.

Clive Porter wiped his hands on his apron, shook his son's hand and smiled at Stella. 'And, this must be Stella.'

Stella noticed he had the same disarming smile that had melted her heart when she'd first met Shaun.

'Pleased to meet you, Mr Porter,' said Stella, accepting his hand.

'Please, call me Clive.'

'Hello, Grandpa,' said Sarah.

Clive swept Sarah into a bear hug and wanted to hear all about her law studies.

'Let's go and find Mum,' said Shaun. 'These two will be talking law all afternoon.'

Before they could move, Erica Porter appeared with a dish full of meat for the barbecue. 'Thought I heard you arrive.' She put the dish on the table next to the barbecue and hugged Shaun. 'You're looking good.'

'Mum, this is Stella.'

Erica smiled and embraced Stella. 'Finally, we get to meet you. Welcome.'

'Pleased to be here, Mrs Porter,' said Stella.

'Call me Erica. No need to be formal here.'

Stella decided she liked Shaun's mother, and watched as she embraced her granddaughter and asked her about her life at university.

'Open that bottle of red while I get this meat on,' said Clive, pointing to the bottle of Shiraz on the table next to the meat. 'Will you have a glass, Stella?'

'Stella's another member of the white wine club, Dad. I've brought a bottle of Mum's favourite Chardonnay with me for the girls,' said Shaun.

'Don't tell me you drink that lolly water too, Sarah,' said Clive.

'I'll be sticking with water, Grandpa,' said Sarah.

Clive pulled a face. 'Don't see what people see in that stuff.' He shook his head. 'Can't see the point in drinking something that has no taste.'

'You've spent too many years in the Clare Valley, Grandpa,' said Sarah.

'Well, when in Rome, a man's got to do what the Romans do,' said Clive, taking the glass of Shiraz Shaun offered him.

'Isn't this place known for its white wines, Grandpa?' said Sarah.

'No need to get into the fine detail, young lady. They make a lot of nice reds here.'

Shaun opened the Chardonnay and poured glasses for Stella and his mother.

Stella went inside with Erica and Sarah and left Shaun to talk with his father while he cooked the meat.

'I like your garden, Erica,' said Stella, as they sat around the table in the family room.

'Gives me something to do,' said Erica.

'You sound like my father,' said Stella. 'He's always working in his garden when he's home.'

'Is your father retired?'

'No. He's still working, but he's had a garden for as long as I can remember.'

'Do you like gardening?'

'I like being in the garden but I haven't done any gardening for a long time. Guess I'm spoilt with Dad looking after it for me.'

'Shaun's good with plants. He had a nice garden in Melbourne,' said Erica.

'I can't even get him to buy a pot plant for the apartment,' said Sarah.

'Perhaps we can fix that,' said Stella, 'by buying him a few.'

'Might work if you do it,' said Sarah.

'You two aren't ganging up on poor Shaun are you?' said Erica, elbowing Sarah in the ribs.

'Someone has to look after him,' said Stella, 'and, we only have his best interest at heart, don't we, Sarah?'

The back door opened. 'What are you lot laughing about?' said Clive.

'Oh, nothing,' said Erica.

Clive placed the dish of cooked meat on the table. 'Time to eat.'

Shaun came in with their wine and joined them at the table. Erica supervised the distribution of the food and it wasn't long before they were enjoying their meal.

'So, what are your intentions, Stella? Are you going to give Shaun here a run for his money or turn him into an honest man?' said Clive.

'I didn't know he had any money,' said Stella.

Clive laughed.

'Behave yourself, Clive,' said Erica. 'You'll be giving Stella the wrong impression.'

'Too late for that,' said Shaun. 'She's already met me.'

'I've been trained to make my assessments based on the evidence and not let first impressions cloud my judgment,' said Stella.

'So, there's hope for me yet?' said Clive.

'Depends,' said Stella. 'Shaun's grown on me and I guess he got his charm from someone in this room.'

'Yes, well we know who that would be,' said Erica, 'and, it definitely wasn't me.'

Clive winked at Stella.

'So, how are you enjoying retirement, Clive?'

'It's certainly improved my golf,' said Clive.

'Bloody well hope so,' said Erica. 'You spend enough time following that little white ball around the course.'

'Doing anything apart from playing golf, Dad?' said Shaun.

'Rotary. That keeps me out of mischief and your mother's hair.'

'What do you do with your spare time, Stella?' said Erica.

'Family, mostly. Apart from spending time with Josh, I spend a lot of time with my parents and my brother's family when I'm not at work or working out to stay fit.'

'Where is Josh today? You could have brought him with you,' said Erica.

'Football,' said Stella. 'I'm trying to persuade Shaun to come out and watch him play.'

'Round ball,' said Shaun.

'You can go a long way in soccer these days. Is he any good?' said Clive.

'My brother thinks so,' said Stella, 'and he used to play for Adelaide City.'

'And, what's he think of your relationship with Shaun?' said Erica.

Stella put down her fork and knife. 'He was five when his father died so, as you can imagine, we're pretty close but he's been good about Shaun coming onto the scene, wouldn't you say, Shaun?'

Shaun nodded. 'He's a good kid.'

'What do you think, Sarah?' said Erica.

'He's a boy,' said Sarah, shrugging her shoulders.

After lunch they sat around talking about life in Clare. Clive told stories of Shaun's boyhood exploits that had them all laughing and Erica coaxed a few similar stories from Stella. By four in the afternoon, when they were saying their goodbyes and getting ready for the return trip to Adelaide, Stella knew she'd been accepted as Shaun's new girlfriend.

There were no handshakes when they were leaving. It was hugs all round.

CHAPTER 5

AT EIGHTEEN MINUTES to three on Wednesday afternoon, a white van with Australia Post signage pulled into the parking bay in front of the Brompton Post Office. The surveillance team watched the driver climb out of the van, open the sliding door in the side of the van, and then carry a cardboard box into the post office.

The surveillance team verified that the tracking device in the box was operational and then sent a text message to Sergeant Tim Wilde.

The delivery had been made. In the listening post, they waited.

Ten minutes after the Australia Post courier left the post office, the listening team heard Andrew Knight tell Mark Roberts that the pens had arrived and that he would deliver them after work.

The message was relayed to DI Williams. He gave the order to go.

Brian parked the car in the bay vacated by the Australia Post van that had delivered the parcel.

'Looks like Wednesday is a slow day down here,' said Stella, as she surveyed the almost empty car park.

'We have the rear sealed,' said a voice over the radio.

A patrol car pulled in alongside them and two armed officers wearing body armour climbed out of the car and walked into the post office.

Stella picked up the radio hand piece. 'Going in.'

'Police! Put your hands in the air!'

Stella walked in behind them and approached Knight, who was standing behind the counter in the rear of the shop with his hands in the air.

'Don't even think about it, mate!' said Brian, when Knight dropped his hands.

'What the fuck's going on?' said Knight.

'Where's the parcel that was just delivered?' said Stella.

'What parcel?'

'No need to play dumb, Mr Knight. We know it was delivered.'

Andrew Knight stared at Stella but didn't respond. Tim had warned her he wouldn't cooperate as he'd feel bound by the so called bikie code of honour.

Brian walked through into the room behind the counter that serviced the post office boxes.

'It's in here.'

He came out carrying a cardboard box addressed to Mr A Einstone, PO Box 304 Brompton SA 5007, Australia.

'You know what's in here, don't you, Mr Knight?' said Stella.

'It's not addressed to me, so why would I know what's in it, you stupid bitch!'

'Watch your language, sunshine,' said Brian.

'I'll say what I fucking want, you old fart!'

'So, if you don't know what's in the parcel, why did you tell your friend Mark that you'd deliver his pens after work tonight?'

Knight looked at Stella. She saw the realization dawn in his eyes.

'Have you bastards been listening to my phone calls?'

'That's what happens when you break the law, Mr Knight,' said Stella.

'I haven't broken any of your stupid laws.'

'When was the last time you spoke to Mr Einstone?' said Stella.

Knight remained silent.

'You may as well know, we know what's in the box, Mr Knight, and it's not only technical drawing pens like it says on the customs declaration form.'

'It's not my parcel,' said Knight.

'Oh, so who is Mr Einstone?' said Stella.

'How the fuck would I know?'

'Do you have his contact details, seeing as he has a post office box here?'

'I want to speak to my lawyer.'

'Pat him down, Brian. I want his keys,' said Stella.

Brian checked Knight's pockets and relieved him of his keys.

'Andrew Knight, I'm arresting you for possession of a prohibited import,' said Stella. 'Anything you say will be taken down and may be used in evidence against you.' She turned to the armed officers. 'Take him away, boys.'

One of the armed constables pulled Knight's hands behind his back and handcuffed him, and then led him out of the post office.

After Knight's departure, Stella closed the post office and called Henry Withers.

'Mr Withers, this is Detective Sergeant Bruno. I'm calling to inform you that I've arrested the manager of the Brompton Post Office.'

'What?'

'I've arrested Andrew Knight, Mr Withers. I'd like you to send someone over who can help me find out who Post Office Box 304 is leased to,' said Stella. 'Mr Knight didn't want to tell me.'

'Just a minute, I can do that from here.'

Stella heard the sounds of a keyboard clicking.

'That's a vacant box, Sergeant. It's not leased to anyone.'

'Can you send someone to lock up? I'm currently searching the premises, so if you could have someone here by four, that would be good.'

'I'll come over myself.'

By the time Henry Withers arrived, Stella and Brian had searched the backroom of the post office without finding anything of interest.

'Mr Withers, would you mind telling me how you met Andrew Knight?' said Stella.

'He was introduced to me by a friend of one of my sons,' said Mr Withers. 'I know he's a bit of a rough diamond, Sergeant, but we've had trouble keeping someone in this shop. Andrew's been great since he started with us a couple of years ago.'

'Are you aware he's a member of a bikie gang?' said Stella.

Mr Withers looked at the floor. 'What he does in his own time is none of my business, Sergeant.' He looked up and smiled. 'I was more than happy with his performance.'

'Did you know he'd served time for assault?'

'I knew about that but I was prepared to give him a chance. He'd served his time.'

Stella wished there were a few more people like Henry Withers who were prepared to give someone a second chance after he'd served his time. Too bad Knight had let him down.

'Well, it looks like he may have abused your trust, Mr Withers. We've arrested him for importing guns through this post office.'

'Are you sure it was him?' said Mr Withers.

'I don't think he's acting alone but I'm sure he's involved.' Stella made to leave and then stopped. 'You don't by any chance know of someone by the name of Einstone, do you?'

Stella watched the colour drain from Henry Withers' face.

'That's my younger son Thomas' nickname.'

'I'd like to speak to him,' said Stella.

'He's overseas, in Germany.'

'Oh, when will he be back?'

'I'm not sure he'll be coming back any time soon, Sergeant. He's married to a German girl and she doesn't like it here.'

'Was it one of Thomas' friends that introduced Andrew to you, Mr Withers?'

'Yes. Doug Watson. He was in the army with Thomas.'

'How long has your son been in Germany, Mr Withers?'

'It'll be two years, next month.'

'Do you know where he lives in Germany?'

'They live with her parents on a farm somewhere near Munich. Thomas works for her father.'

Stella arrived at the house in Coglin Street as Julia Mahoney was getting out of her car in the driveway. She watched as a police car pulled into the driveway behind Julia's car and blocked her exit.

'Let's go, Brian.'

They walked along the driveway to where Julia Mahoney was standing next to her car holding a pile of exercise books and her handbag.

'Are you Julia Mahoney?' said Stella.

'Yes. What's going on?'

Stella pulled out her ID. 'Detective Sergeant Bruno. We're here to search this house.'

Julia looked at the four officers standing in front of her. 'Why?'

'I understand you share this house with Andrew Knight, the manager of the local post office. Is that correct?'

Julia nodded. 'He should be home soon.'

'Andrew won't be coming home tonight, Ms Mahoney. He's been arrested.'

Julia dropped several exercise books before she managed to regain control of the pile in her arms by clutching it to her breast.

'Here, let me hold those for you,' said Brian, picking up the spilled books and taking the pile from her.

'We have a warrant to search the house,' said Stella, 'and, I have Andrew's keys.'

'His bike is in the shed,' said Julia. 'I can let you into the house.'

'How about you take us in and show us around?' said Stella.

Stella sat with Julia in the kitchen while Brian and the two officers searched the house, the yard, and the shed housing Andrew Knight's motorcycle.

'What's he been arrested for?' said Julia.

'He's been smuggling guns into the country through the post office,' said Stella.

'Andrew? I don't believe it. You'd need more brains than he's got to arrange something like that.'

Stella wondered what sort of relationship Julia had with Andrew Knight.

'We don't think he was acting alone. Do you know someone called Mark Roberts?'

'He's one of Andrew's friends. They go riding together on

weekends.' Julia looked up. 'They reckon they're bikies but they're all talk. Mark's got a wife and three kids.'

'Do you go riding with them?' said Stella.

'I don't like motorbikes,' said Julia. 'They make too much noise for me.'

'Do you know Doug Watson?'

'Yes. He's a friend of Einstone's. They were in Afghanistan together.'

'So, you know Einstone?'

'Yes, he was at school with Andrew and my brother.'

'How does someone called Thomas get a nickname like Einstone?'

Julia smiled. 'Tommy's not someone you'd called a genius in the academic sense, Sergeant. Boys can be cruel.'

Stella nodded. She'd reprimanded her own son for talking about some of his school friends in ways she didn't approve of.

'His father told me he'd married a German girl.'

'Yes, a nurse he met in Afghanistan. She's really cute. Not sure what she sees in Tommy but they seemed to be in love when they were here.'

At six fifteen, Brian came into the kitchen.

'Nothing here, Sarge.'

Mark Roberts' motorcycle repair shop was one of several workshops in the industrial estate on Acrylon Road, Salisbury South. Mark and his three employees were standing outside the office at the front of the building smoking and drinking coffee when Tim Wilde and his raiding party of heavily armed officers arrived.

The four men exchanged glances and stood their ground as the police poured out of their vehicles and pointed weapons at them.

'You boys sure you're at the right address?' said Mark. 'There's nothing going on here.'

Tim Wilde walked up to Roberts. 'We're at the right address, Mark.'

'Look who's here, boys. It's Timmy from the Bikie Taskforce.' Mark flicked his cigarette ash towards Sergeant Wilde. 'No bikies here, mate. Only bikes.'

'We're here to search the place, Mark.'

'Can I see your search warrant?' said Mark.

Tim handed the search warrant to Roberts to read.

Mark read the page and tore it in half before handing it back to Tim. 'Doesn't look legal to me, mate.'

His companions laughed.

'Up against the wall and spread your legs!'

The four men turned and slowly complied. Once they'd been patted down, they were herded into the workshop and ordered to sit on the floor with their hands on their heads.

Sergeant Wilde stood with the officer guarding the four while the rest of his men searched the premises.

'In here, Sergeant!'

Tim Wilde walked into the office where one of his men stood next to a metal toolbox.

'It's locked.'

Tim returned to the workshop and walked over to Mark Roberts.

'Where's the key to the green toolbox in your office?'

Roberts shrugged his shoulders.

Tim walked back into the office. 'Get the bolt cutters.'

When the officer snapped the lock and opened the lid they were looking at twenty-five partially built Glock pistols wrapped in oilcloth.

Tim returned to the workshop. 'Cuff 'em!'

As the four were being handcuffed, the sound of motorbikes

filled the air. Tim spun around and watched as a group of bikies blocked the driveway out of the repair shop. He counted six and could hear the sound of more approaching. He reached for his radio.

'Tango One. I need that back up, now!'

'On its way, Tango One.'

More bikies joined the group in the street in front of the workshop. One of them rode his machine into the yard. He was armed with a semi-automatic rifle, which he pointed over the handle bars of his bike in Tim's direction.

'Time for you and your girls to piss off, copper!'

'Put down that weapon, mate,' said Tim.

The bikie didn't appear to notice the red light of the laser sight illuminating a spot on his chest.

'This is not worth getting killed over,' said Tim.

'Fuck you!'

He levelled the rifle at Tim and fell backwards as the round fired by the policeman standing in the workshop's office hit him in the chest. The rifle discharged into the clouds as he hit the ground. His bike toppled with a clatter.

Police cars with flashing blue lights appeared at the intersections at both ends of Acrylon Road.

The bikies in the street looked at each other, then throttled up and scattered but there was no way out of Acrylon Street and nowhere to hide from the police dogs. The sound of roaring motorbike engines died.

Tim Wilde sprinted over to the man on the ground. He was still alive. Tim reached for his radio. 'Tango One. I need an ambulance. Gunshot wound to chest.' Then he did what he could to stop the bleeding.

The thudding of the police helicopter overhead was the only sound until the wail of a siren announced the arrival of the ambulance, but it was too late for the man on the ground.

More police vehicles arrived.

The bikies were taken into custody along with Mark Roberts and his employees.

Tim Wilde sat in one of the patrol cars and called DI Williams.

'We've got twenty-five partially built and five operational Glocks, Inspector, and a little problem.'

'What do you mean, Wilde?'

'I've arrested ten of the blokes we were going to raid tomorrow, and shot one dead.'

'What the hell happened?'

'We were ambushed at Roberts' repair shop. One of the stupid bastards tried to shoot me. Five of the others were armed with Glocks.'

'How the hell did they know you were there?'

By the time Stella arrived at work on Thursday morning, the raids on the homes and businesses associated with the Mongrels were winding down. As the reports came in, it was obvious the previous day's events had blown any element of surprise they might have had. No more guns were found.

At midday, DI Williams called Stella.

'Bruno, we need to find out who's behind this little operation. Let's see if we can get Knight and Roberts to tell us anything.'

Stella set up the interviews and they waited for Patrick Mahoney, who was representing both Knight and Roberts, to arrive.

At two fifteen, Stella followed DI Williams into the interview room where Andrew Knight sat waiting for them with his lawyer.

'Andrew, things are not looking good for you, mate,' said DI Williams. 'Importing prohibited firearms is a pretty serious crime, and you've been caught red handed with the goods, so to speak. Not a good look.' DI Williams stopped speaking and leant back in his chair.

Andrew Knight looked at his lawyer but said nothing.

'Things might go a little easier for you if you tell us who else was involved.'

'You're full of bullshit,' said Andrew Knight.

'What my client is saying, Inspector, is that he doesn't know anything about the guns you claim he imported,' said Patrick Mahoney. 'He simply works in the post office that the parcel was addressed to and, as you know, it wasn't addressed to him.'

'That may be his story but I'm not buying it. Who else is involved, Andrew?' said DI Williams.

'My client can't tell you things he has no knowledge of, Inspector,' said Patrick Mahoney.

Stella thought that was a clever answer. Maybe it was true that Knight didn't know who was behind the operation and that he was just a cog in the wheel.

'Who's Einstone?' said DI Williams.

Andrew Knight looked up but said nothing.

'I understand you both went to school with Thomas Withers.' DI Williams looked from Andrew Knight to his lawyer.

Patrick Mahoney smiled. 'Who told you that, Inspector?'

'Thomas's father,' said DI Williams.

'Then, it must be true,' said Patrick Mahoney.

'Do you remember if Thomas had a nickname?' said DI Williams.

'I always called him Tom,' said Patrick.

'That's not what I asked,' said DI Williams.

'I always called him a dickhead,' said Andrew. 'He was nuts.'

'Couldn't have been too crazy, Andrew. He served with the SAS.'

Andrew Knight shrugged his shoulders.

'I understand it was one of Thomas' army mates that got you the job in the post office?'

'Doug? Yeah, he persuaded old man Withers to give me a go. Not many people are willing to give you a go once you've been inside. More than Thomas ever did for me.'

'How do you know this Doug Watson? You haven't done any time in the army.'

'He's a member of the club. We go riding together on weekends.'

'He didn't put you up to this little caper, did he?'

'My client isn't involved in any little caper, Inspector. I think you've got your story wrong,' said Patrick.

DI Williams folded his arms and rested them on the table. 'I find it a little strange that your parcel was addressed to someone called Einstone, especially since his father told us that was Thomas's nickname.'

'The world's full of strange coincidences, Inspector,' said Patrick Mahoney, 'but that doesn't prove my client knows anything about why this one occurred.'

Stella felt Mark Roberts' eyes undressing her when she entered the interview room with DI Williams, and focused her attention on Patrick Mahoney as she took her seat opposite Roberts at the table that separated them.

'Things are not looking good for you, mate,' said DI Williams. 'Possession of a prohibited import is a pretty serious offence all by itself, but importing and selling prohibited firearms, is a hell of a lot more serious. You're probably looking at ten to fifteen years.'

Mark Roberts shrugged his shoulders.

'The Court might look at you more favourably if you coop-erate with our investigation and tell us who else was involved.'

'I've got nothing to say to you.'

'What was Andrew Knight's role in your little operation?' said DI Williams.

Mark Roberts looked at his lawyer. 'Dumb shit, isn't he?'

'My client has admitted to importing the guns with the intention of selling them, Inspector. There is nobody else involved.'

'How many guns exactly have you imported?'

'I assume you dumb fuckers can count,' said Mark Roberts.

'How many besides the ones in the box?'

Mark Roberts folded his arms.

'My client only arranged to get those twenty-five guns into the country, Inspector.'

'I find that hard to believe,' said DI Williams, 'seeing we have recovered more than twenty-five Glocks.'

'Guess my client must have competition,' said Patrick Mahoney. 'Isn't that the way the market works?'

Another smart-arse answer, thought Stella.

'What's your relationship with Doug Watson? Did you sell him a Glock?' said DI Williams.

Mark Roberts smiled. 'If Doug's got a Glock, he didn't get it from me.'

'So, you know Doug Watson?'

'I'm sure your mate Timmy has told you who's in our motorcycle club, so why are you asking me something you already know? Don't you trust Timmy?'

'How do you explain five other members of your so called motorcycle club having Glocks on them when they showed up at your workshop yesterday?'

Roberts shrugged his shoulders. 'Guess you'd better ask them. They didn't get them from me. You've seen my pistols. I needed that last shipment to put them together so I could sell them.'

'Are you saying you haven't actually sold any?'

'How could I? You busted me before I got the last shipment.'

DI Williams leant back in his chair. 'How do you think we traced that shipment to you, Mark?'

Roberts shrugged his shoulders. 'How the fuck would I know?'

'Do you think we got lucky at Customs? Got any idea how many parcels come into the country from overseas? Maybe you do, which is why you took the risk. Well, let me tell you we didn't get lucky. We knew your package was coming.'

Mark Roberts looked at his lawyer.

'What are you saying, Inspector?' said Patrick Mahoney.

'I'm saying your client isn't telling us the whole truth, Mr Mahoney. I'm saying your client has imported and sold into the community an unknown number of prohibited firearms, including the five seized during yesterday's raid.'

'You can say what you like,' said Mark Roberts. 'It doesn't prove anything.'

'What's your evidence, Inspector?' said Patrick Mahoney 'and how is it linked to my client?'

DI Williams opened the folder he had placed on the table, took out a piece of paper and handed it to Patrick Mahoney. 'This is a photograph of a Glock pistol we recovered from a vehicle involved in a collision with a Stobie pole. The driver was killed but not before he'd used this pistol to shoot a pensioner.'

'What's that got to do with my client?'

'That pistol has different serial numbers on its three main parts.'

Stella noticed that Patrick Mahoney's eyes flicked to Mark Roberts before he returned his attention to DI Williams. 'What does that mean?'

'It means the gun was put together from parts. It wasn't purchased as a complete unit, which is how Glock sells them.'

'I still don't see how this has anything to do with my client, Inspector.'

'We asked Glock who they'd sold the guns with those serial numbers to, Mr Mahoney, which is how we came to be sitting here today. They sold the guns to the dealer that shipped that box of parts to your client.' DI Williams smiled. 'I think that means your client has imported more than twenty-five pistols and has sold them.'

'Fair amount of conjecture there, Inspector.'

'I don't think the Court will see it as conjecture, Mr Mahoney. It's a logical sequence of events that our German friends will corroborate.'

DI Williams turned back to Mark Roberts. 'Your last chance to cooperate, Mark. Who else was involved?'

'Fuck off!'

CHAPTER 6

TIM WILDE JOINED Stella and DI Williams in the inspector's office when they returned from interviewing Mark Roberts.

'Any luck with any of your interviews, Wilde?' said DI Williams.

'No-one is saying anything. They're all copping the charge.'

'Bikies code of honour or something?'

'Shit scared of what will happen to them if they spill the beans, more likely,' said Tim.

'Anything on the one that got himself shot?'

'I'm waiting on the toxicology report. One of the lads I interviewed told me Sims was a meth user. Said he couldn't believe he'd actually pulled a gun on a bunch of armed policemen. Reckoned he must have been out of his mind.'

'Either that or he had a personal vendetta against you, Wilde.'

'Either way, sir, he got himself killed for no good reason.'

Stella smiled to herself. She liked the way Tim handled DI Williams.

'Why were they even there?'

'Sending us a signal, I'd say. Letting us know we can't touch people like Roberts without the rest of them knowing.'

'What does that say about Knight? Nobody turned up when we arrested him.'

'Says he's not part of the hierarchy. He's a foot soldier, not a general.'

The inspector rubbed his chin. 'So, it's possible Knight's a pawn in someone else's game?'

'I'm not so sure he's a pawn, sir, going by what we heard on the intercepts.'

'What do you think, Bruno?'

'I think we need to trace the money trail. I reckon that might tell us who's behind the scheme, and I'd like to know more about this Doug Watson. He might be the missing link.'

'What makes you think that?'

'He's the one that got Knight into the post office. He's a former soldier, so he'd know about weapons, and he belongs to the Mongrels. And, his kid brother had a Glock on him when he was arrested for holding up that service station.'

'Wilde, why don't you bring him in for a chat?'

'I'll have some of the boys meet him at the airport. I think he's due to fly in tomorrow morning.'

'And, Bruno, I want you and Rhodes on that money trail.'

Stella watched Doug Watson through the two way mirror while she waited for DI Williams to arrive. He was chatting with the constable waiting in the room with him and Stella thought he looked very relaxed for a man sitting in a police station.

DI Williams arrived and they went into the interview room.

'Thanks for coming in, Mr Watson. I'm hoping you might be able to help us with our enquiries,' said DI Williams.

'And, what enquiries would they be, Inspector?'

'I'm looking into a gun smuggling operation, Mr Watson.'

Doug Watson sat up. 'Oh, and what makes you think I'd be able to help you, Inspector?'

'One of the people involved is Andrew Knight. I understand you helped him get his job.'

'Andrew Knight? Smuggling guns? You're pulling my leg, aren't you?'

'Afraid not, Mr Watson.'

'You'll have to remind me, Inspector, which job did I help him get?'

'Managing the Brompton Post Office.'

Doug Watson smiled. 'Ah, that's right. There's a little story behind that. You see, I served with a bloke called Tom Withers in Afghanistan. He worked in that post office when he got out.' Doug spread his hands in front of him on the table. 'It's not a real post office, it's one of those post office shops. Belongs to Tom's Dad.' Doug shook his head. 'Poor Tom. Fell for this German nurse he met in Kabul. She came out here a couple of years ago to be with him but she didn't like it here, so he had to find someone to take over the post office. That's when he asked me if I knew anybody who was looking for a job. I knew Andrew was looking for work, so I introduced him to Tom. What a laugh! Turns out the buggers went to school together. That was enough for Tom's Dad to give Andrew a go.'

'How did you meet Andrew?'

'Motorbikes. I joined a club when I came out of the army. He's one of the regulars on our weekend runs up into the Barossa.'

'Is this club the Mongrels?' said DI Williams.

'Nah. They're a bunch of lunatics, but I'm sure you know that already. I don't have time for any of that shit. I'm into motorbikes for the enjoyment. It's my relaxation, that's all.'

Stella noticed that Watson was still very relaxed.

PETER MULRANEY

'Do you know Mark Roberts? Runs a motorbike workshop in Salisbury.'

'Yeah, he services my bike.'

'How well do you know him?' said DI Williams.

'Went to school with him.'

'I understand he's a member of the Mongrels.'

'All I know is he's a good mechanic, and I like doing business with people that know what they're doing,' said Doug. 'If he wants to run with the Mongrels, that's his business.'

'Looks like he's into gun smuggling, as well,' said DI Williams.

Doug Watson shrugged his shoulders. 'What can I say?'

'You're not surprised?'

'If there's a buck in it, nothing those guys do would surprise me, Inspector. Why do you think I joined the army? Why do you think I'm working at Roxby?'

DI Williams opened his folder and slid a piece of paper across the table to Watson. 'Do you know what this is?'

'Looks like a Glock.'

'Seen this one before?'

'I've seen plenty of Glocks, Inspector. What's so special about this one?'

'Your brother had it on him when he was arrested after holding up the Caltex Service Station on Salisbury Highway.'

Doug Watson shook his head. 'Yeah, Mum told me about that. In fact, that's what I thought you wanted to talk to me about, but if you think that's my gun, sorry to disappoint you. I don't own a pistol and, if I did, I certainly wouldn't leave it anywhere near a kid with his problems.'

'That must be a concern.'

'It is for Mum. She's worried about what will happen to him, but he won't listen to me. I told him that shit would do his head in. Maybe some time inside will do him good.'

'I doubt that will do him any good,' said DI Williams, gathering his papers.

'Tell me, Mr Watson, why would the Bikie Taskforce think you are a member of the Mongrels?'

'A few blokes I went to school with are in that club, Inspector, and I have a drink with them at the Salisbury every now and then when I'm home, so I guess someone's made an incorrect assumption.'

Stella went through her notes from the interviews with Brian.

'What do you think, Brian?'

'You know, Sarge, Thomas Withers could be the mastermind.'

Stella looked at him.

'Think about it. He knows about the post office. He's in Germany, and that's where the guns are coming from. He could pay in cash and there'd be no trail.'

'Surely he'd want his share of the profits?'

'Then, we should be able to find a trail from Roberts or Knight back to him,' said Brian.

'You're assuming they're using their own accounts. What if all the money is cash and isn't going through the banking system?'

'How else could they get money to him in Germany?'

'What if he took the cash with him when he left? Can't be all that much to buy twenty-five Glocks,' said Stella.

'They're around six or seven hundred euro a piece if bought legally. Who knows how much they'd be on the black market? Probably twice that amount. He'd need twenty-five to fifty thousand euro or more.'

'Be a bit of a risk taking that much cash with you,' said Stella.

'I've been reading up on that. There are no restrictions on taking cash out of the country but you're supposed to report it if you're carrying more than ten thousand dollars. It's no big deal if you can explain where the money came from. And, the European Union has similar rules, so he'd have to declare it the other end if he had more than ten thousand euros on him.'

Stella thought about Brian's hypothesis. Some of it made sense but she had her doubts about Thomas Withers being involved.

'Not sure I buy it, Brian. What's his connection to Knight and Roberts? What's his motive? If what Watson told us is correct, it sounds like Withers was not close to Knight and didn't know Roberts.'

'What if they've got something on him? You know, some dirt that he doesn't want his girlfriend or his father to know about.'

'Okay, let's pencil that in as a possibility and follow up with AUSTRAC to see if he made a declaration when he left the country.'

Stella waited while Brian made a note on the whiteboard.

'What if it's not him? How else can people get money out of the country if they don't use the banking system?'

'I guess they could use a money transfer service like Western Union,' said Brian.

'I remember using Western Union to send money to my brother when he lost his credit card in Italy,' said Stella. 'There'd be a trail we could follow. The person the other end has to identify themselves with a passport or identity card. We could get the police in Munich to search from that end to see if the gun dealer received his payment that way, and then we could trace it back to whoever requested the transfer this end.'

'Do you know how many transfer services there are, Sarge?'

'Let's start with Western Union. If I remember correctly, you can set up a transfer with them at the post office. Be perfect for our boys.'

'Of course, they could have sent a courier with smaller amounts,' said Brian.

'God, they'd have to charge a fortune for the guns or they wouldn't make any money doing it that way,' said Stella.

'You're assuming profit as a motive, Sarge. What if it's only about getting guns into the country?'

'Then why did someone like Allen, who wasn't a member of the Mongrels, end up with one of their guns? They were doing it for money, Brian. No-one smuggles guns just so his mates can have one. There will be a money trail and we will find it, even if we have to get the Germans to look for it their end, because you can bet your boots that gun dealer wasn't doing it for love.'

Stella discussed their money theories with DI Williams.

'AUSTRAC might be a long shot, Bruno, but I guess it's worth a try,' said DI Williams.

'I'm not sure Withers is our man, sir. Can't see his motive. From what we know he's not connected to the Mongrels,' said Stella.

'Well, after our little chat with Watson, I've asked Wilde to review his intelligence sources. We might not know as much about the Mongrels as we think we do.'

'Watson could have been lying to us, sir.'

'I suspect Watson might have told us the truth. I've just had a call from Elizabeth. Your mate Simon Murray's been told by young Watson that he got the gun from Garry Sims, the clown that got himself shot by Wilde's people. Apparently, he was the kid's supplier, and the kid owed him money. Sims gave him the gun and told him to go get the cash or face the consequences.'

'Guess we'll only have the kid's word for that, since Sims is dead,' said Stella. 'It could be a story concocted by Watson to cover his tracks.'

'That's why I've got Wilde reviewing his sources on Watson. Anyway, we'll let Wilde sort that out. I suggest you get on to Western Union. That sounds like a possibility to me.'

Stella arranged her warrants and sent requests to AUSTRAC and Western Union.

AUSTRAC replied within forty-eight hours and informed her that they had no records connected to Thomas Withers.

Western Union provided a list of the transactions initiated at the Brompton Post Office over the last two years that soon had Brian excited.

'Look at this, Sarge!'

'What have you found, Brian?'

'Since Knight took over the post office, there have been fifteen cash transactions of around eight thousand dollars each sent to a Wilhelm Boch in Munich.' Brian looked up from his screen. 'That's the name of the gun dealer, and guess who sent them?'

'Roberts?'

'No, someone called Allen. Greg Allen of Andrews Road, Elizabeth Downs to be precise.'

Stella looked at Brian. 'That's our Greg Allen.'

'Yeah, but he was dead when the last transaction went through,' said Brian ' so it's possible they were using his details without his knowledge.'

'And, who authorised the transactions?'

'Knight.'

'Think we might just have thrown a spanner into his not guilty plea, Brian.'

'Think you're right, Sarge. We've got the bastard!'

Stella ran the figures through her head. 'Shit!' she picked up her phone and called DI Williams.

'We've got the Western Union data, sir. Looks like Knight sent around ninety thousand dollars to that dealer in Munich.'

'That's a lot of money, Bruno. Any idea where that money came from?'

'It's recorded as cash. And, it definitely didn't come from Knight's bank account, and there's no sign it came from any of Roberts' accounts either. In fact, the details of the sender are recorded as Greg Allen, the same Greg Allen that triggered this case.'

'So, was he the mastermind?'

'I think it's more likely he was the patsy, given that the most recent transaction is dated a week after his death,' said Stella.

'I guess the money could be the proceeds of crime' said DI Williams.

'Maybe,' said Stella, 'but that's not why I called, sir. Ninety thousand bucks would buy a lot of guns. Definitely more that the thirty or so we've found so far.'

CHAPTER 7

STELLA SET up interviews with Andrew Knight and Mark Roberts and their lawyer in the Remand Centre to discuss her new evidence. She took Brian with her to the interviews.

'Mr Knight, this is a print out of the Western Union transactions conducted at the post office you manage.' Stella slid the pile of papers across the table so he could read them.

Patrick Mahoney picked them up and scanned them. Andrew Knight said nothing.

'There are fifteen transactions sending money to a Wilhelm Boch in Germany,' said Stella, 'that the German police have confirmed is the gun dealer who sent the Glocks in the package you received.'

Patrick Mahoney ran his finger down the page of the top sheet and nodded.

'All of those transactions were by someone called Greg Allen, and each one was authorised by you, Mr Knight.' Stella looked at Andrew Knight. 'We've checked the driver's licence number you recorded as Allen's form of ID on the most recent transaction on that list.'

Andrew Knight looked at his feet.

'It belongs to the same Greg Allen that was killed in a car accident a week before that transaction took place. How do you explain that?'

Andrew Knight said nothing.

'What's even more interesting, Mr Knight, is he's the one that led us to you.'

Andrew Knight remained silent.

'Something else to think about, Mr Knight, is that these records tell us you started sending money to Germany within six weeks of taking the job. And, all those transactions add up to more than ninety thousand dollars, which suggests you're involved in an organized gun smuggling operation involving more than the twenty-five guns in that package.'

'Do you think I could have a moment with my client, Sergeant?' said Patrick Mahoney.

'If you think it will help, Mr Mahoney.'

Stella and Brian stepped out into the corridor to allow Patrick Mahoney to confer with his client.

'Do you think he'll crack, Sarge?' said Brian.

'I'd say he's currently losing the support of his lawyer,' said Stella, 'and that he's being advised to come clean.'

The interview resumed five minutes later.

'My client has changed his story somewhat, Sergeant,' said Patrick Mahoney.

'Would you like to elaborate, Mr Knight?' said Stella.

'I admit, I sent the money.'

'Why did you use Greg Allen's driver's licence number?'

'Greg gave it to Mark as part of the deal for getting one of the pistols. The little shit wanted to be part of the group so much he did anything Mark asked him to do.'

'Where did the money come from? I know it didn't come out of your bank account.'

'You'll have to ask Mark that. He gave it to me. My role was to send the money and collect the packages when they arrived. I had nothing to do with selling them.'

'What was your cut?' asked Stella.

'Two hundred dollars for every pistol we got in,' said Andrew Knight.

'How many did you get in?'

Andrew Knight looked at his lawyer. 'Seventy-five counting the last lot.'

'All Glocks?'

'Yeah, all Glocks.'

'Anybody else besides you and Roberts involved?'

'I really have no idea. I took my orders from Mark.'

'What about Doug Watson?'

Andrew Knight shook his head. 'I met Doug on a weekend ride into the Barossa and we got to talking. He'd just come out of the army and was looking for a job. I told him how I was finding it hard to get a job because of my record.' Andrew looked at his hands. 'A couple of months later he told me he had a friend that was looking for someone to manage a post office, and that friend turned out to be Einstone. Small world, hey?' He looked at Stella. 'Doug's not even a member of the group. I think he only comes on rides because he went to school with Mark and some of the other boys.'

'Who's idea was it to use the post office to smuggle in the guns?'

'That was Mark's idea. He came up with it after he'd been to Europe for a holiday.'

'Why did you agree to be involved?'

Andrew Knight shrugged his shoulders. 'Mark can be very persuasive.'

After ending the interview with Knight, Stella rang DI Williams.

'Knight's confessed to being involved. Claims they've imported seventy-five Glocks.'

'Did he cough up anybody else?'

'He only mentioned Roberts. Said he was the brains behind it all,' said Stella.

'What did he say about Watson?'

'His story lines up with Watson's account.'

'Okay. Good work, Bruno. See if you can get anything else out of Roberts.'

Stella went into the interview with Mark Roberts after Patrick Mahoney had conferred with his client.

'I take it you're aware that Andrew Knight has changed his story, Mr Roberts?' said Stella.

'So what?' said Roberts.

'I think it might have implications for you, Mr Roberts,' said Stella.

'You can think what you like, sweetheart. Doesn't change anything for me.'

'Not sure I'd agree with you there, Mr Roberts. According to Andrew Knight, it looks like your little operation has been more successful than you're prepared to admit. If my maths is correct, there are still forty-three Glocks out there somewhere,' said Stella.

'Well, they didn't come through my hands.'

'Are you suggesting Andrew Knight was operating on his own, Mr Roberts?'

'How the fuck would I know? All I know is I only got twenty-five guns and you lot got them before I could do anything with them.'

'Knight says you supplied the cash for all seventy-five,' said Stella.

'Then he's a liar, sweetheart.'

'He also told me you sold a Glock to Greg Allen,' said Stella.

'Good try, sweetheart, but I haven't sold a Glock to anyone.' Mark Roberts opened his hands in front of himself. 'How could I? You lot have all the guns I imported.'

Stella decided she was wasting her time. It was obvious Roberts wasn't going to change his story and was happy to let Knight take as much blame as he could send his way.

'We need to get someone who had one of the guns to talk,' said Stella, as they made their way out of the Remand Centre.

'We've got five guys to work on,' said Brian.

'Are any of them still here?' said Stella.

'They all got bail,' said Brian. 'We'll have to get them brought in. Fat chance the Inspector will let us go visit.'

'Well, that was a waste of time,' said Brian, as he and Stella watched the last of their five bikies leave after giving them the same answer his colleagues had given them.

'They know how to stick to a script. Got to give them that,' said Stella.

Brian laughed.

'What's so funny?'

'I bought it from a bloke at the Salisbury. I didn't ask him his name. Nah, I couldn't identify him. It was dark.' Brian grinned at Stella. 'I wonder how long it took them to learn their lines.'

'I wonder why none of them want to finger Roberts. After all, he's confessed to importing the guns we found at his workshop. What's the hold he has over them?'

'Fear and retribution,' said Brian. 'That's been the bikies' code as long as I've been on the job, Sarge.'

'If Roberts will be inside for ten years or more, why are they afraid of him?'

'It's not Roberts they're scared of. You have to remember that these guys belong to a national organisation. That retribution could come from anywhere, not just Roberts.'

'So, those pistols could be anywhere.'

'Certainly wouldn't surprise me if the first batches went interstate, where the big boys are,' said Brian.

'Guess I'd better tell DI Williams we got nothing out of these guys.'

Stella sat in the chair in front of DI William's desk.

'I've got two confessions but neither is complete. Knight's admitting to sending the money and receiving the guns but denying he's either the mastermind or the banker. He's given those roles to Roberts, who's only admitted to importing the twenty-five weapons we seized at his workshop.'

'That should be enough to send them both away for years,' said DI Williams.

'What I'd like to know, sir, is who's got the other Glocks? We've only recovered thirty-two of them, and both Knight and the Germans have confirmed they imported seventy-five of them. That's forty-three unaccounted for.'

'I've had Wilde pass on that information to his counterparts interstate. He thinks they're most likely in New South Wales, where the Mongrels have their headquarters.' DI Williams stood and walked around to where Stella was sitting. 'I'd say the brains behind this operation is neither Roberts or Knight, which is why they'll only implicate each other and no-one else if they want to stay alive.'

'When do you want my report, sir?'

'I'm meeting with the DPP on Friday. Can you have it ready by then?'

'Yes, sir.'

Andrew Knight and Mark Roberts went into the criminal justice system to await the determination of their fate, which would depend not only on their willingness to plead guilty and talk about their operation but, in an overloaded system with a backlog of cases, also on the availability of a judge to hear their case.

In faraway Munich, Wilhelm Boch was arrested for gun running and Thomas Withers was cleared of any suspicion of being involved.

In Adelaide, Stella completed her report and waited for her next assignment, which she knew wouldn't be long in coming.

On Friday evening, Stella met Shaun at Georges on Waymouth to celebrate the closing of the investigation.

'What are you drinking?' said Shaun, as Stella joined him at the table he had reserved.

'I'll have a Chardonnay.'

Shaun raised an eyebrow. 'You catching a cab home or something?'

'I was thinking of the or something,' said Stella, fluttering her eyelashes.

Shaun smiled. 'Should I get a bottle?'

'That would be nice. I don't have to work this weekend.'

Stella looked at the menu while Shaun ordered their drinks.

'Let's have the sharing board of appetisers,' said Stella, when he returned to the table.

'Are you feeling hungry?'

'I'll let you know after we've tried the appetisers.'

The waiter arrived with their drinks and Shaun ordered a sharing board of appetisers.

'Here's to you, Detective Sergeant. Nice work.'

'I take it you've read our report then?'

'Yes, I met with Frank this afternoon. He was pretty excited. You'd think he'd won the lottery.'

'Well, it's not every day you catch the bad guys red handed and they confess,' said Stella.

'Not very bright boys, I'd say,' said Shaun.

'They were smart enough to work out how they could use the postal system to get guns into the country without too much trouble.'

'I'll give them that, but we still don't know whether it was their idea or not. And, I gather we're not likely to find out either. No, what I meant was they could easily have avoided detection.' Shaun picked up his glass of wine. 'All they had to do was remove the serial numbers, and Roberts probably had the equipment to do that in his workshop.'

Stella sipped her wine and thought most criminals were never as smart as they thought they were.

'I guess we wouldn't have suspected an organized smuggling operation if they'd simply been a little more careful putting their Glocks together. It was the mixed serial numbers on the gun in Allen's car that made us sit up and take notice,' said Stella.

Shaun shook his head. 'So, what have you got planned for the weekend?'

Stella put her glass on the table. 'Oh, I was thinking about spending it in bed with a man.'

Shaun's face lit up with that smile that Stella couldn't resist.

'What have you done with Josh?'

'He's gone to Melbourne with Rick's parents for the weekend. They're taking him to watch the Reds play Melbourne Victory.'

'That's very considerate of them,' said Shaun.

Stella took another sip of her wine. 'Yes, and Sarah is spending the weekend in Clare.'

'Is she? She didn't say anything to me.' Shaun put down his glass. 'How's she getting there?'

Stella smiled. 'In my car.'

BONES IN THE FOREST

STELLA BRUNO INVESTIGATES

A few Australian terms:

Bullocky (bullockies) Australian term for bullock driver.

Country Fire Service is the volunteer service that fights bushfires in rural South Australia

TAFE Colleges are public, fee-based colleges of Technical and Further Education that deliver trade based courses.

CHAPTER 1

It had taken Stella and Brian three hours to drive from Adelaide to Wirrabara in the mid-north of the state, where the local constable was waiting for them at the Wirrabara Police Station. After a comfort stop, they followed his patrol car out to the Wirrabara Forest Reserve, several kilometres west of the town, and then along narrow dirt tracks through a burnt-out pine forest to where a group of vehicles was parked.

The overpowering smell of burnt pine trees hit Stella when she stepped out of the car. As she looked around, she could see wisps of smoke snaking their way towards the clear blue sky. Stella thought she'd stepped into an alien landscape.

They walked over to where Forensics' crime scene investigators had cordoned off the area around the skeleton, which had been discovered by a local Country Fire Service crew conducting mopping up operations after the bushfire that had ripped the life out of the pine plantation.

Stella felt unnerved by the deathly silence of the place. It was the first time she'd been in a forest immediately after a fire where there were none of the usual sounds of nature. The only sound she could hear as they walked was the crunching of burnt pine needles under their boots.

'This place is giving me the creeps,' said Brian.

'Know what you mean.'

They stopped at the line of crime scene tape and waited for Dr Steve Wright, the forensic pathologist, to walk over and join them.

'Hello, Steve,' said Stella.

'Nice day for a drive, Stella.' He smiled. 'How are you, Brian?'

'I'm good, Doc,' said Brian.

Stella pointed to the skeleton lying on the ground less than three metres from where they stood. 'What's his story? What makes you think he's not a camper that forgot to wake up?'

'The holes in his skull. There's one above the eyes and a larger one at the back. Whoever this guy was, Stella, he didn't die in his sleep,' said Steve.

'Any sign he was camping here?'

'We've looked for tent pegs and metal utensils but haven't found anything. To be honest, I'm more inclined to think he was probably shot somewhere else and dumped here.'

'What makes you think that?'

'See those burnt sticks on top of the skeleton? I'd say they're what's left of whatever was used to hide the body from view.'

Stella pictured a body under a pile of fallen branches some twenty metres from the nearest track. Steve's hypothesis sounded plausible.

'Any idea how long he's been here, Steve?' said Stella.

'We'll have to wait until we can get one of the guys from the museum to analyse the bones back in the lab. I'm afraid the fire has made it impossible to guess with any degree of certainty.'

Stella nodded. 'Have you found anything that might suggest this is at least from our lifetime?'

'Not yet.'

They walked back to their car where the local constable was waiting.

'Any likelihood he's a local?' said Stella.

'Pretty tight knit community here, Sergeant. Whoever he is, he's not from around here.'

'This might take a while,' said Brian, as they got back into the car and followed the local constable back into Wirrabara.

They ate lunch at the Wirrabara Hotel and listened to the buzz of conversation among the locals discussing the find in the forest. After lunch they returned to Adelaide, as there was little they could do until they had some idea who the skeleton belonged to and some expert had confirmed it was not from the ancient past.

Steve Wright asked Dr Malcolm Edwards, a forensic anthropologist attached to the South Australian Museum, to analyse the bones recovered from the floor of Wirrabara Forest to determine their age and how long they'd been in the forest.

After examining the bones and conducting a series of tests to determine how long they had been exposed to the elements, Dr Edwards advised that the skeleton belonged to a young adult male who had died somewhere between five and ten years ago.

After studying the holes in the skull in his laboratory, Steve Wright confirmed his original opinion that, whoever he was, the young man had died as a result of a gunshot wound to the head, and that the dimensions of the entry wound were consistent with a round fired from a twenty-two calibre rifle. He also advised Stella that access to the victim's dental records would give them a good chance of identifying him, as the skull contained a complete set of teeth and its lower jaw appeared to have been fractured at some point.

Stella reviewed the list of long-term missing persons in the database. There were six potential candidates in the South Australian list and considerably more in the national list.

She looked at the names on her list of missing South Australians and imagined each of the six families waiting to find out what had happened to their son. If the bones belonged to one of them, she realized that family would be devastated and the others would be traumatised by the experience of reliving their loss. Stella wondered how she could minimize the amount of trauma those families would have to endure as she read through the summary of each case.

Five of the young men on her list had gone missing from Adelaide or one of its suburbs. One person on the list, however, nineteen-year-old Mark Semmler from Spalding, had gone missing five years ago after a football game in Clare, which was a little over a hundred kilometres from Wirrabara.

Stella read the Semmler case notes. Mark Semmler's disappearance was described as suspicious and unresolved. According to the file, his abandoned car had been found in the car park of the Clare Hotel, the day after he'd failed to return home from playing football in Clare on the afternoon of Saturday the twenty-fifth of June, 2011. Although his wallet and mobile phone had been found in the car, it appeared he'd taken his keys with him.

The file detailed the extensive public appeal conducted at the time. Stella noted that it had failed to elicit any sightings of Semmler after he'd left the dining room of the Clare Hotel, around eight pm on the night he'd disappeared, to drive home to Spalding.

After reading the file, Stella decided she'd contact Pam Ross, Mark Semmler's mother, who had reported him missing, and wondered how much of the media's reporting of the finding of bones in Wirrabara Forest had reached her. She looked through the file again and located Pam Ross' mobile phone number.

'Mrs Ross, Detective Sergeant Bruno from Major Crimes in Adelaide. Are you somewhere we can talk in private?'

'This is about those bones from Wirrabara, isn't it? I wondered when I'd hear from you. Is it Mark?'

Stella noted that her voice was matter of fact, without any obvious emotion.

'We don't know who the bones belong to yet, Mrs Ross, which is why I'm calling. Do you remember who your son's dentist was?' said Stella.

'He went to the clinic in Burra. There's only the one.'

'I'll give them a call.'

'Will you let me know?'

Stella thought she could hear a note of desperation in her voice.

'Yes, Mrs Ross I'll let you know as soon as I find out, one way or the other.'

Pam Ross had been dreading the call ever since she'd seen the item about the bones in Wirrabara Forest on the TV news. She'd been tempted to call the police herself and ask but hadn't been able to muster the courage. She'd wanted to hold on to the hope that Mark was still alive out there, somewhere, and would come home to her.

The supermarket was empty. Pam went outside for a smoke and wondered whether she should call Grant and let him know the police had called. But, after thinking about it, decided she'd rather not speak to him. She didn't want to hear him blaming her again for being a bad mother to their son.

Grant blamed her for Mark's disappearance and, on the few times they had spoken since Mark had gone missing, had taunted her with his claim that if she'd been a better mother Mark wouldn't have run away from her. In fact, when she thought about it, she realized Grant had blamed her for everything that had upset him during the twenty years they'd spent together.

She wrapped her arms around her thin body and remembered the beatings. She could almost feel the pain of his fists hitting her, and had to remind herself that she'd finally had enough of being his punching bag and had found the courage to leave when Mark was fifteen. Four years before he went missing.

It had been Mark's choice to come with her when she'd returned to her home town. He'd been afraid of the violent man his father had become. In fact, he'd only started speaking to his father again in the year before he went missing. By then, he'd left school, started work as an apprentice motor mechanic in Spalding, and become part of the local football team.

Pam blew a stream of smoke into the air. Mark had been football mad ever since he'd discovered the game in primary school, and she'd been all over the mid-north as a football mum in his teenage years.

It was only when Mark had started playing senior football that Grant had shown any interest, loudly boasting of his son's prowess on the field. Pam had stopped going to the games when Mark had bought his car. She couldn't stand being in the same space as Grant and his new woman.

A picture of a jeering Grant appeared in her mind.

'Fuck you, Grant!'

Pam turned her thoughts to Peter, whom she'd married the year after Mark had gone missing. He was nothing like Grant. He was kind and considerate, and had never once hit her in anger.

She flicked the end of her dead cigarette into the dust at her feet and went back into the supermarket to tell Peter about the call. She found him in his office.

'I've just had a call from the police about that skeleton they found at Wirrabara.'

Peter looked up from the inventory report on his desk. 'Do they think it could be Mark?'

'They don't know. They wanted to know who his dentist was.'

Peter stood and walked around to where Pam was standing and put his arms around her. 'You okay?'

Pam had no idea where the tears were coming from but she couldn't stop them and let them flow.

'Do you want to go home?' said Peter. 'I can look after the shop.'

Pam found a tissue in her apron pocket and dabbed at her eyes. 'I just want it to be over, Pete. I don't know that I can take much more of this not knowing.'

Shortly after his thirteenth birthday, Mark Semmler had received a kick to the face during a game of football that had broken his lower jaw and resulted in extensive work being done on his teeth at the dental clinic attached to the Burra Hospital.

The records of that dental work enabled Dr Wright to identify the skeleton found in Wirrabara Forest, and he called Stella as soon as he'd confirmed the skeleton was Mark Semmler's.

Stella, relieved she had made the right call, contacted Pam Ross and advised her that they had identified the skeleton from Mark's dental records.

'What happens now?' said Pam.

'Now we work out what happened to him,' said Stella.

'What do you mean?'

'It's a murder investigation now, Mrs Ross. Your son was shot in the head.'

Stella heard Mrs Ross suck in a deep breath.

'I guess that explains why he didn't come home. I knew he wouldn't stay away by choice.'

'I'm sorry, Mrs Ross,' said Stella.

'Well, at least I can stop waiting for him to call now. When will I be able to bury him?'

'Ask your funeral director to call the Coroner's Office, Mrs Ross. They'll tell them when they're ready to release Mark's remains and where to collect them.'

Pam ended the call and slid down the wall until she was sitting on the floor of the kitchen. Her whole body felt numb. She'd thought she was going to cry when she heard they had identified the bones as being Mark's but no tears had come. She was surprised at how calmly she'd taken the news.

In one way it was a huge relief. She'd felt a weight lift from her heart when she heard he was dead and not hiding from her. She'd never believed he'd run away from her, despite what Grant had said. Now, as she sat on the floor, icy fingers gripped her heart and her tears began to flow and tumble into sobs of grief.

Her mobile phone trilled beside her on the floor. Pam looked around. She wasn't sure why she was sitting on the floor or how long she'd been there. She picked up her mobile and answered it.

'Are you alright, honey. You sound dreadful,' said Peter Ross.

'The police called.' She sniffed as she fought to control her voice. 'It's Mark.'

'Oh, I'm so sorry, honey,' said Peter.

'They're saying he was murdered. Shot in the head.'

'Shit! Who'd do that?'

'I don't know.'

'Do you want me to come home?' said Peter. 'I can get Beryl to watch the shop.'

'I think I'd like to have some time alone,' said Pam.

'I understand. I'll call you later.'

Pam went into the living room and pulled Mark's photograph album from the bookcase and flipped through its pages. She couldn't believe she'd never see him again. She stared at the last photograph in the album, a picture of Mark in his football gear, which she'd taken the day he'd first played in the A Grade team.

Seeing all the photographs of Mark with his father made her think of the good times they'd had together as a family, before Grant's dark demons had surfaced. She thought of Grant and wondered if the police had called him.

She picked up her mobile and called his number. He answered on the third ring.

'Hello, Pam.'

Pam thought he sounded flat and wondered how she'd sound to him.

'Have the police called you, Grant?'

'Yeah. Just now, before you called.'

'Did they tell you they think he was murdered?'

'Yeah. They said they'd be coming to interview me again.'

'Me, too.'

'I don't know what to say, Pam. I never expected this.'

'Will you come to his funeral service?'

'Of course. When is it?'

'I'll let you know.'

CHAPTER 2

CASSIE KING WATCHED Grant Semmler walk into the front bar of the Burra Hotel. She liked the way he carried himself, as if he was in command. For a man approaching fifty, he was in good shape. She'd decided he was hers for the taking the first time she'd seen him. Since then, she'd done her research and confirmed he'd be open to her type of service. When he'd taken a seat at the bar, she opened the top two buttons of her shirt and walked over and sat next to him.

'Want to buy a girl a drink?'

Grant turned and looked at her, and wondered why she'd picked him. She let him look down her blouse at her braless breasts. Grant decided he liked what he could see. He moved his eyes back to her face. 'What's in it for me?'

Cassie smiled and placed her hand on his crotch. 'When was the last time you had a good fuck?'

Grant hadn't had a fuck of any type in the two years since Pam had left him. 'What are you drinking?'

Cassie knew she had him where she wanted him. 'I'll have a beer, thanks.'

Grant ordered two beers and took another look at her. He guessed she couldn't be older than forty.

'So, what brings a girl like you to Burra?'

'Adventure.'

Grant cocked an eyebrow. 'Adventure?'

'I hear you're a roo shooter. I've always wanted to kill something. Could you teach me how to shoot kangaroos?'

Grant sipped his beer. 'Can you cook?'

'Sure.'

'Well, if I enjoy fucking you, I'll teach you to shoot a kangaroo in exchange for you cooking me something.'

'Oh, you'll enjoy being fucked by me.' Cassie picked up her glass and drank her beer.

'Where are you staying?'

'Upstairs.'

Grant thought about going upstairs with her and decided that probably wasn't a good idea.

'Perhaps we should go out to my place. It's much quieter out there.'

Cassie smiled. That was what she had planned all along. 'That sounds like a good idea.'

'Do you have a name?'

'Cassie. Cassie King.'

'I'm Grant. Grant Semmler.'

'I know,' said Cassie. 'I don't just fuck anybody, Grant.'

Grant downed the rest of his beer and wondered how she'd known who he was, and just what she'd meant by her comment.

'How long are you planning to be in Burra, Cassie?'

'That depends on you, Grant.'

Grant looked at her. She wasn't a beauty but she wasn't ugly by a long shot, and she had great tits. He was aroused just looking at her and thinking about what it would feel like to touch her.

'Shall we go?'

Cassie picked up her bag and linked her arm in his. She let

him escort her out to his car and drive her to his house, located a little over three kilometres north of Burra.

'You need more than a cook,' said Cassie, as she surveyed the interior of Grant's house. 'You need someone to pick up after you.'

'Yeah, well I've been on my own for the last couple of years.'

'Got any clean sheets?'

'In here.' Grant opened the linen press in the corridor outside his bedroom and took out a clean set of sheets and pillow cases.

'Let me help you change the bed,' said Cassie.

When she had smoothed down the clean sheets and changed the pillow cases, Cassie turned to face Grant and unbuttoned her blouse, before slipping it off. Then she took off her jeans and dropped her knickers, before walking over and helping him remove his clothes.

Grant thought he was in control but things didn't go as he'd planned. First, she took him in her mouth, then she worked him over so that when he came again, he had no idea she'd faked her orgasm.

Around midnight, she cooked him a meal and then took him back to bed.

In the morning, he asked her to stay. She acquiesced, and asked him to drive her back into town so she could check out of the hotel and get her car.

Cassie spent the rest of the day helping him clean the house and inserting herself into his life.

By the end of the first week she'd spent with him, she'd taken possession of his desires and seduced him into submission. By the end of the month, he'd taught her to shoot and introduced her to the world of kangaroo shooting.

Cassie was a natural with a rifle but it was her butchering skills that helped her become an essential part of Grant's operation.

Stella read the case notes made by the team that had investigated Mark Semmler's disappearance.

Mark had been reported missing by his mother on Sunday, the twenty-sixth of June, 2011, the day after he had failed to return from playing football in Clare. According to the interview notes, his mother had expected him home around nine on the Saturday night and had tried to contact him when he had not arrived by ten. She'd called the police in the morning when she awoke and discovered he wasn't in the house and wasn't answering his mobile phone.

The local police had found his car in the car park of the Clare Hotel. When they'd opened the car, they'd found his wallet and mobile phone in the console between the front seats and a sports bag with his dirty football gear in the boot.

They'd established that Mark had joined some of his team mates for dinner in the dining room of the Clare Hotel after the game, and had left to drive home around eight. James Paterson, one of his team mates, had told them that Mark's car had not been in the car park when he'd left to drive home at eight thirty.

The investigators had interviewed Grant Semmler, Mark's father, and his partner, Cassie King, as they had been at the game on the Saturday. They'd told the investigators they'd had a drink with Mark in the pub after the game and then driven home and gone kangaroo shooting that night. They were each other's alibi, as no-one could confirm what they'd done after leaving the Clare Hotel, as Grant's shooting territory was located in the remote emptiness north-west of Burra and they lived on a property three kilometres north of the town.

It seemed Mark Semmler had simply vanished. According to the lead investigating officer, no-one appeared to have a motive to harm him, and his behaviour was totally out of character. The lead investigator had suspected foul play when Mark failed to return or access his bank account, and had sought public assistance to locate him.

One page of the report detailed the breakdown of the relationship between Mark's parents, and included a list of the domestic violence complaints Pam Semmler had made in the years leading up to the time she'd left her husband and taken their son with her in 2007. Mark's parents had divorced in 2008, three years before he'd disappeared.

Grant Semmler had admitted to the investigators that he and Pam had had a rocky relationship and told them he'd sought help for anger management before reaching out to re-establish a relationship with his son when he'd turned eighteen.

The lead investigator had noted that Pam and Grant Semmler were not talking to each other and had not communicated since their divorce.

The case had been kept open for months but, with no leads or information from the public to work with, it had soon become a cold case and the investigators had moved on to other active cases.

Stella went over the case notes with Brian.

'What do you think, Brian?'

'I'm putting my money on the roo shooter.'

'Why's that?'

'Ever been roo shooting, Sarge?'

Stella shook her head. 'Not something that's popped up as an opportunity, Brian.'

'They shoot them through the head.'

Pam Ross opened the door and led Stella and Brian into her living room.

Stella noticed a glass-fronted cabinet holding numerous sporting trophies opposite her as she sat down at the table in the centre of the room.

'Are they Mark's trophies?' said Stella.

'No, they're mine,' said Pam.

'Oh, what sport are you involved in?' said Stella.

'Small bore rifle shooting. I used to be pretty good at it,' said Pam. 'Made the Australian team for the 2000 Olympics but I don't do much of it these days.'

'Did you win a medal?' said Brian.

Pam shook her head. 'I wasn't that good.'

'Was Mark interested in shooting?' said Brian.

'Funny, isn't it? Grant and I are both shooters. That's how I met him. But Mark wasn't interested in guns. He certainly wasn't interested in shooting kangaroos, which is what we did for a living.'

'Know what you mean,' said Brian. 'None of my kids is interested in policing.'

'Tell us a bit about Mark, Mrs Ross. What was he like?'

'He was one of those kids that liked to pull things apart and put them back together again. If you gave him anything, the first thing he did was pull it apart. He always wanted to know how things worked.'

'That must have been frustrating for you,' said Stella.

'Especially when he'd put something back together and it wouldn't work,' said Pam.

'How did he react to that?'

Pam smiled. 'He'd just keep working on it until he'd fixed it.'

'Is that why he decided to become a mechanic?'

'I guess so. He wasn't all that interested in school and when Peter's brother offered him an apprenticeship at the end of year 11, we all thought it was for the best.'

'Did he have a girlfriend?' said Stella.

'Nothing serious. They're weren't that many girls his age around here. I think he was sweet on a girl he met in Clare. Someone he met when he was at the TAFE College doing the school part of his apprenticeship.'

'Do you know this girl's name?' said Stella.

'Let me get his album,' said Pam.

'Okay.'

Pam got up and walked over to the bookcase behind Stella and pulled out a photograph album. When she returned to the table, she opened the album and turned the pages until she found the one she wanted. 'This is his TAFE class.' She turned the album so Stella could see the photograph. 'That's Mark there,' she pointed with her finger, 'and that's Michelle.'

Stella looked at the group photograph of apprentice motor mechanics and noticed that there was only one girl in the group. 'Do you remember her last name?'

'Williams,' said Pam, 'but I guess she could be married by now. I only ever met her once. She came to see me after Mark had disappeared.'

'Oh, why was that?'

'She was the girl he'd been talking to in the pub that night. Said he'd promised to meet her at TAFE on the Wednesday of that week. Apparently, they were working together on some group assignment.' Pam shook her head. 'Poor girl, she couldn't understand why he would disappear like he did and, to be honest, neither could I.'

'Do you mind if we take a copy of that photograph?' said Stella.

'Go ahead,' said Pam, passing the album to Stella, who handed it to Brian.

Brian took the photograph out from behind its protective plastic sheet and photographed it with his iPhone, and then carefully replaced the photograph.

'Did Mark have any friends apart from the people in this group?' said Stella.

'The boys at the football club,' said Pam.

'I have a list of their names from the initial investigation.' Stella took the list from her folder and placed it on the table. 'Are any of them still playing football?'

Pam looked at the list. 'I don't know about that,' said Pam, 'but most of them are still living here. The only ones that wouldn't be would be the boys from the bank and the school. Most of them only stay for a couple of years.'

'What about James Paterson? Is he a local?' said Stella.

'Yes. He's taken over the family farm. His father had a stroke, poor man. He's paralysed down his right side.' Pam shook her head. 'In fact, I think James got married last year.'

'I know you've probably been asked this before, but can you think of anyone Mark may have upset?'

'He wasn't that sort of kid, Sergeant.'

'How did he get on with his father?'

Pam leant back in her chair. 'I guess you know about the domestic violence,' said Pam.

Stella nodded. 'It's mentioned in the case notes.'

'Mark was scared of his father. Grant never abused him but he did witness some of Grant's outbursts,' said Pam. 'That's why he was living with me.'

'Was he in contact with his father at all?'

'Grant was making an attempt to reconcile with him.' Pam smiled. 'He'd been to see his father a few times in Burra but he never stayed long. I think both times they met for lunch and talked. The other development was Grant had started showing up to watch him play football.'

'Do you think his father could have killed him?' said Stella.

'What would make you think that?'

'The way he was shot,' said Stella, 'through the head.'

Pam Ross stood and walked over to the window and looked out at her garden.

'I've thought a lot of bad things about Grant, Sergeant, but never that. He might have been a bastard when he'd had too much to drink but deep down he's a decent person.' She turned and looked at Stella. ' I never would have married him if he hadn't been.'

Stella stood and closed her file. 'One last question, Mrs Ross. Where were you on the night Mark disappeared?'

'I was working in the kitchen at the pub in those days. Saturday nights were our busiest, especially during the footy season. I didn't get home until ten that night. That's when I tried to call Mark.'

Pam Ross stood at the window of the living room and watched the detectives get into their car and drive away. She found her cigarettes and went out and sat at the table on the back veranda and lit up. Peter didn't approve of her smoking in the house.

She wondered whether the police knew something she didn't. That question about whether Grant could have killed Mark worried her. She hadn't thought about that possibility, and shooting kangaroos through the head was something Grant did on a regular basis. God, she'd shot plenty of them herself when she'd been with him.

She sucked in a lungful of smoke and slowly blew it out into the air. Grant had loved Mark, and had been heartbroken when Mark had decided to live with her instead of stay with his father. Grant might not have spoken to her after their divorce but he had tried to keep in contact with his son. Pam couldn't imagine Grant wanting to harm Mark, let alone kill him, but the thought of the possibility wouldn't go away.

How would they prove it if he had, she wondered. How could they work out who had killed Mark five years ago when no-one had come forward with any information when he had disappeared.

She stubbed out her cigarette in the ashtray on the table and stared at the trees in the yard without seeing them. It dawned on her that even though she now knew Mark would never be coming home, her anguish would never end if they couldn't work out who had killed him.

The house telephone rang. She went inside and picked up the receiver.

'How did it go?' said Peter.

'I don't think they know anything about who killed Mark, and I doubt they'll ever find out,' said Pam. She looked at the clock on the kitchen wall and realized she'd better do something about going to work. 'I'm on my way.'

'Let's go and see Dave Ross,' said Stella. 'His workshop is in the main street.'

Brian started the car and retraced their path to the main street of Spalding.

'What did you make of his mother?' said Stella.

'There was nothing in the file about her being a marksman,' said Brian.

'Well, no-one knew he'd been shot then.'

'Perhaps we should consider her a suspect as well.'

'Only if we think she had someone else abduct him, Brian. The case notes confirm what she told us about being at the pub. There's a statement from the manager of the hotel and one from the other kitchen hand. Besides, what would be her motive?'

'What would his father's motive be, Sarge, if what she told us about him is true?'

'Some of these domestic violence situations get pretty bizarre, Brian. He wouldn't be the first bloke to do something to the kids as a way of getting to his ex,' said Stella.

'He'd have to be a spiteful bastard to kill his son four years after they split up, wouldn't he?'

'Some of these guys never let go, Brian. It's that place over there.'

Brian parked in front of Dave Ross Motors.

Dave Ross walked out from the workshop as they were getting out of the car.

'I guess you're the police,' said Dave, extending his hand.

'Detective Sergeant Bruno,' said Stella, shaking his hand. 'This is Detective Constable Rhodes.'

'What can I do for you?' said Dave.

'As I mentioned on the phone, Mr Ross, we're investigating the murder of Mark Semmler. We'd like some background information on Mark.'

'He was a good kid, Sergeant. Good with engines, too. He had a bright future here.'

'How long did he work for you?'

'Nearly three years. I took him on at the end of 2008, when he finished school.'

'Any issues you think we should be aware of?'

'What sort of issues?'

'Friendship tensions, drug or alcohol abuse, anything like that?'

'Not that I'm aware of. He was never late for work. In fact, I had to tell him to knock off. Not like my other apprentice at the time.'

'Oh, who was that?'

'My son, Greg.'

'How did they get on?'

'They were great mates. Played in the same footy team. Chased the same girls.'

'So, was your son one of the lads in the Clare Hotel with Mark the night he disappeared?'

'No. He came home with me straight after the game,' said Dave. 'It was my wife's birthday.'

'Do you know Mark's father, Mr Ross?'

'Grant? Yeah, I've known him for years. He used to come here when he was chasing Pam and beat us all at darts. The bastard's a top shot with a rifle. No wonder he took on roo shooting.'

'Were you surprised when Pam divorced him?'

'I was more bloody surprised when she married him, to be honest.'

'Oh, why was that?'

'He was a control freak but she couldn't see it. I tried to warn her but she told me I was only jealous', said Dave.

'Why would she say that, Mr Ross?'

Dave looked at his boots. 'We'd been an item before she met Grant but I couldn't compete. He was her hero when it came to shooting. I was just an apprentice mechanic working for my Dad. And, I wasn't into guns.' Dave looked up and shook his head. 'There was no way I was going to be an Olympic shooter.'

'I take it Mark wasn't into guns either?'

'Another reason we hit it off. No, we were interested in fixing things, not putting holes in them.'

'Is your son about?'

'He's out servicing a harvester over by Booborowie, but I doubt he'd be able to tell you anything about Mark I don't know, Sergeant.'

After speaking with Dave Ross, they drove to the local police station to interview James Paterson, who'd volunteered to come in and meet them instead of trying to direct them to his farm.

'Tell us about the night Mark disappeared,' said Stella.

'A few of us went to the pub in Clare after the game. We'd been thrashed, so there was no fear of anybody giving us a hard time. If we'd won, we'd have come back to Spalding, but I think Mark would have gone to the pub even if we'd won.'

'Oh, why's that?'

'He had a girl with him when he joined us in the dining room.'

'Was that Michelle Williams?' said Stella.

'Yeah. She was doing the same course as Mark at Clare TAFE but I think they may have been more than classmates, if you know what I mean.'

'What made you think that?'

'She was practically sitting in his lap until the food was served,' said James.

'Did Mark drink much that night?'

'Mark didn't drink, Sergeant. He was only having lemon squashes.'

'Did Michelle leave when Mark did?'

'Yeah. He walked her out to her car around eight. Said he'd be heading home after that.'

'I see from the statement you made at the time that you claimed his car was not in the car park when you left half an hour later,' said Stella.

'I'd parked my car next to his. His car definitely wasn't there when I left. Someone must have parked it there later, unless he'd returned to the pub after I'd gone home.'

'Think we can assume someone else returned his car to the car park now,' said Stella. 'Do you know if Michelle Williams is still in the area? We might need to talk to her.'

James rotated his hat between his hands. 'She's out in the car, if you'd like to talk to her. We're married.'

'Why don't you ask her to come in?'

Stella and Brian waited while James Paterson went out to fetch his wife.

'How did you two get together?' said Stella, when Michelle and James were seated.

'I was doing farm management at the TAFE in Clare. I guess we supported each other after Mark disappeared, and things sort of developed from there,' said James.

'How long have you been married?' said Stella.

'We got married last December,' said Michelle. 'My mother wasn't keen on me marrying a farmer, especially one that lives out in the middle of nowhere.'

Stella smiled. 'Mrs Paterson, we won't keep you long. Can you tell us what happened when you and Mark Semmler left the Clare Hotel the night he disappeared?'

'He walked me to my car and promised he'd have his part of the assignment finished by Wednesday. He kissed me, and then watched me drive out of the car park. That's the last time I saw him.'

'Was your car parked anywhere near his?' said Brian.

'I was parked close to the door. He told me he was parked just inside the entrance to the car park. I drove past his car on the way out.'

'Notice anyone standing near his car or just outside the car park?' said Stella.

'Not that I recall.'

'Had you ever been inside Mark's car?' said Brian.

'He'd driven me home from TAFE a few times before I got my own car.'

'Was it usual for him to put his wallet and mobile phone into the slot in the console between the seats?'

'It was the first thing he did when he got into the car. I know they found his wallet in the car, so he must have gotten into his car before whatever happened, because he had his wallet with him in the pub. He paid for my meal. Makes me wonder who enticed him out of the car if he didn't take it with him.'

'Good question,' said Brian. 'Any suggestions?'

'Makes me think it must have been someone he knew or someone who'd asked him for help. He was always helping people.'

CHAPTER 3

STELLA READ the notes from the interviews Grant Semmler and Cassie King had given to the initial investigators in the thirty five minutes it took Brian to drive them across country from Spalding to Burra.

They grabbed a quick lunch at the Burra Bakery and then followed the directions Grant had given them out to his house.

Semmler's house was at the end of a long driveway lined with gum trees. When they reached the end of the driveway they found themselves in a dirt yard bordered by a house, a shed containing three vehicles, and a cold storage unit with a padlock on its door.

'Man, pretty quiet out here,' said Brian. 'Talk about living in the middle of nowhere.'

'Guess it must have its good points, Brian, but you're right. Too isolated for me.'

A man appeared on the side veranda of the house when they got out of the car and watched as they walked towards him. A black dog walked up to their car, cocked its back leg and marked their hubcaps before returning to the shade under the tank stand.

'Grant Semmler?' said Stella.

'You that detective that rang this morning?'

'Detective Sergeant Bruno,' said Stella, holding out her ID, 'and this is Detective Constable Rhodes.'

'Come inside.'

Stella noticed that he didn't offer to shake hands or acknowledge that he was Grant Semmler, but he looked like the man in the photograph in the folder under her arm.

'Put the kettle on, Cassie. The police are here,' said Grant. 'We can sit in here.'

He led them into the dining room next to the kitchen and pulled out the chairs from the table in the centre of the room.

'What makes you think he was murdered?' said Grant, when they were seated.

Stella opened her folder and took out a photograph of the skull found in Wirrabara Forest. She placed it on the table in front of Grant.

'This is a photograph of your son's skull. Forensics have determined those holes are the result of a gunshot wound, Mr Semmler.'

Grant studied the photograph and shrugged his shoulders. 'There's usually not that much skull left when you shoot a roo, so I guess I'll have to take your word for it.'

A woman came into the room from the kitchen holding a tray with a teapot and four cups.

'This is Cassie,' said Grant. 'She lives with me.'

'Anyone take milk or sugar?' said Cassie.

'Black's fine with us,' said Stella.

'How long have you been in the roo shooting game,' said Brian, while Cassie poured their tea.

'Most of my working life. We supplied the pet food industry in the early days. Now kangaroo is being sold as gourmet meat, which is why that cooler is out there in the yard. We put the dressed carcasses in there and they send a refrigerated truck out to pick them up.'

'What sort of rifle do you use?' said Brian. 'Last time I went spotlighting, we used a twenty-two.'

'I use a Howa twenty-two two-fifty. You want something reliable,' said Grant, 'and I reload my own ammo. The bloody stuff you buy these days is crap.' Grant picked up the cup of tea Cassie had placed in front of him.

'You involved in the business, Ms King?' said Stella.

'He does the shooting. I dress the carcasses,' said Cassie.

'I read somewhere that you have to do a course for that these days,' said Brian.

'That's right, but it was pretty easy. I worked at the Port Wakefield Abattoir before coming to Burra, so dressing kangaroos wasn't a big deal after working on steers,' said Cassie.

'We both had to do a course to kill for the gourmet market,' said Grant. 'It's not like in the pet food days when all you had to know was how to shoot and gut them. Now you need a bloody licence.'

Stella put down her cup. 'Tell us about the day Mark disappeared. I understand you were at the game that day.'

'I was trying to rebuild my relationship with him. I guess you know he'd chosen to go with his mother when she left.'

Stella nodded. 'That must have been hard.'

'Yeah, it was a bit of a shock to realize my own son was afraid of me.' Grant looked at his hands. 'Cassie told me about this anger management course she'd done, so I thought I'd give it a go. Anyway, it helped me reach out and re-establish contact with him. They told me to show an interest in his life if I wanted to be part of it.'

Stella wondered where Cassie would have come across an anger management course and why she'd needed to do one but chose to stay with her line of questioning. 'Is that why you went to watch him play that day?'

'Yeah. He was a bloody good footballer. Had been ever since

he'd started as a junior. Probably could have played for one of those Adelaide teams, if he'd wanted to.'

'Did you speak to him after the game?' said Stella.

'We had a drink with him in the Clare pub after the game but we didn't stay long. We needed to bag another ten roos to meet our quota for that week's pickup,' said Grant.

'What time did you leave the pub?' said Stella.

'A little after six. We were home before seven, and on our way out to the range by eight.' Grant looked at Cassie. 'That sound right to you?'

Cassie nodded her head. 'I think he was distracted that night. He was more interested in his girlfriend than us.'

'Do you recall the girlfriend's name?'

'He didn't introduce her. Said he had to go when she walked into the bar and they went into the dining room together.'

Stella asked Brian to show them the group photograph of Mark's TAFE class on his iPhone.

'Was she the girl in that photo?'

'Looks like her,' said Cassie, passing the iPhone to Grant.

'Yeah. That's her.'

'Apart from each other, is there anyone else who could confirm your movements that night?' said Stella.

'Well, I guess the barman from the Clare pub could confirm when we left the front bar but, as you would have noticed on your way out here, we don't have any near neighbours, and there's no-one out where we shoot roos,' said Grant. 'Why would you want to confirm our movements? You don't think one of us killed him, do you?'

Stella crossed her arms on her chest. 'I don't know who killed your son, Mr Semmler, but my job is to consider all possibilities, and then find ways to eliminate people until I'm left with the killer.'

Grant stood and towered over Stella. 'So, I'm one of your possibilities, then?'

Stella felt the hackles rise on the back of her neck but stopped herself rising to the bait.

'Look at it from my perspective, Mr Semmler. You're a crack shot and you kill kangaroos by shooting them through the head. That puts you on my list of possible suspects. It doesn't mean you killed your son.'

'Well, his mother's a crack shot, too, and she's shot plenty of kangaroos,' said Grant, sitting down.

'I know that,' said Stella, 'however, I need to show that the killer had both a motive and the opportunity to kill Mark before I can get a conviction. So, if someone else could confirm your whereabouts on the night of June the twenty-fifth, 2011, that would eliminate you from my list, as you wouldn't have had the opportunity to either abduct or shoot Mark, especially if that witness could confirm you were nowhere near Clare after eight o'clock that night.'

'Well, I can confirm that,' said Cassie.

'Unfortunately, Ms King, you have a vested interest in confirming his story, as Mr Semmler has in confirming yours. An independent witness would put you both out of the picture, so is there anyone you can think of who might have seen you on the road or driving through Burra?'

Grant shook his head. 'Not many people out at that time of night and, besides, it was dark. But why would I kill my own son?'

'That's the other part of my equation, Mr Semmler. Just because someone might have had the opportunity it doesn't mean that person pulled the trigger.'

'I loved Mark. There's no way I would have shot him.'

Stella gathered her folder and stood. She was ready to leave.

'How many vehicles did you own at that time?' said Brian.

'The same three we have now,' said Grant.

'Which one did you drive to Clare that day?' said Brian.

'We took Cassie's Mazda.'

'Thank you for seeing us,' said Stella. 'I know it can't be easy having to talk about this.'

'He's been gone for five years, Sergeant. I hope you can find his killer but I don't like your chances after all this time,' said Grant.

Stella looked at the three vehicles in the shed as they made their way back to the car.

'Can't be a lot of money in shooting kangaroos.'

'Those Toyota's last forever, Sarge, and it looks like he's one of those Valiant freaks. I wonder how many hours he spends polishing that thing.'

When they got back to Adelaide later in the afternoon, Stella met DI Frank Williams in the coffee shop on the ground floor of Police Headquarters.

'If his father killed him, it looks like he's gotten away with it,' said Stella.

'What makes you think that, Bruno?'

'It's five years since he disappeared and Forensics think he was killed pretty well straight away, going by the state of the bones. Which, when you consider he didn't access his bank account or contact anyone after the day he disappeared, makes sense.' Stella sipped her coffee. 'And, in all that time, no-one's come forward with anything useful. Not one sighting.'

'You think the trail's gone cold?'

'I'm not even sure we have a trail. It's like he walked out of the Clare Hotel and vanished, only to turn up dead five years later at Wirrabara. How did he get there? And, why there? It's over a hundred kilometres from Clare.'

'He obviously didn't drive there himself and I doubt he walked, Bruno. There must be some connection to Wirrabara. If his father shot him, you'd think he would have disposed of the body out there in the middle of nowhere where he shoots kangaroos. It's not like anyone goes out there bushwalking or camping.'

'Maybe that was too close to home, but what if I'm wrong, and someone else killed him?'

'That's a possibility but you need a motive. Maybe young Paterson wanted him out of the way so he could get the girl.' DI Williams shrugged his shoulders. 'From what I've read in the case notes from the original investigation, young Semmler doesn't appear to have made any enemies, but that doesn't mean he hadn't. And, Paterson certainly wouldn't admit to being in competition with him for the girl, would he?'

'Where would you start, Inspector?'

'Wirrabara. See if you can find a connection. If you still think it's the father, see if you can find anyone who might have seen one of his vehicles between Clare and Wirrabara. My guess is he'd have used his four wheel drive if he was planning on venturing into the forest at night.'

'Transporting the body in the same truck he uses to carry kangaroo carcasses would be a good way to hide any blood,' said Stella.

'Keep me posted, Bruno. Be nice to get this bastard.'

Stella joined Brian in the squad room.

'The Inspector thinks we should focus on finding the connection between Semmler and Wirrabara.'

'Which Semmler? Mark or Grant?'

'Perhaps we should look at both,' said Stella.

'I wonder if anyone in that group photograph his mother gave us is from Wirrabara,' said Brian.

'Get on to the TAFE College in Clare and find out. They should have that information.'

Stella reviewed the case notes. According to what he'd told the original investigators, Grant Semmler had lived on the farm outside Burra all his life and, when he wasn't shooting kangaroos, worked with his brother on the family sheep farm. There didn't seem to be anything connecting him to Wirrabara, which was one hundred and ten kilometres north west of Burra.

Brian put down the receiver. Stella looked up.

'Apart from Mark and Greg Ross, all the kids in that class were from Clare.'

'Would Mark have been to Wirrabara to play football?' said Stella.

'Give me a minute, I'll ask Google.'

Stella waited while Brian ran his queries.

'Wirrabara became part of the Southern Flinders Tigers in 2002. They play in the Northen Areas Football Association. Semmler played for the Brinkworth Spalding Redhill Tigers. They're part of the North Eastern Football League, so no, it doesn't look like it.'

'God, is every country football team called the tigers,' said Stella.

'All the ones that are black and gold,' said Brian.

Stella laughed.

'Perhaps we should speak to some people up there now that we know he was murdered. Maybe someone will remember something about that night,' said Brian.

'Good idea. It's not like anybody asked them back in 2011, is it?' Stella looked at her watch. 'Book us a couple of rooms in the Wirrabara Hotel for tomorrow night, and we'll head there first thing in the morning and see what we can find out by talking to the locals.'

Stella called Shaun.

'I'm going to be out of town for a couple of days. Do you want to catch up for a drink?'

'Sorry, Stella, I'm snowed under here. Don't think I'll be getting away any time soon. We've got a big case starting tomorrow. Perhaps we can catch up on the weekend.'

'Okay. I'll give you a call when I get back Friday night. Good luck for tomorrow.'

So much for her irregular hours stretching their relationship, thought Stella. It seemed to her that the office hours of officers working for the Director of Public Prosecutions were also a little irregular, especially when they had a big case on hand.

Stella called Josh.

'How was your day, honey?'

'It was okay. I'm doing my homework. I've got a math's test tomorrow.'

'Do you need anything from the supermarket?'

'Can you get me some toothpaste, Mum. I forgot to add it to the list this morning,' said Josh.

'Okay, I'll see you in about an hour. I'm just on my way to the shops.'

Supermarket shopping wasn't one of Stella's favourite activities but buying the things Josh needed and the food that became part of the meals they shared with their extended family gave her a sense of being a responsible mother and family member.

When she was in the butchers, she noticed they were selling prepackaged kangaroo meat.

'Is that popular?' she said, pointing to a tray of kangaroo fillets. 'I met a bloke today who shoots kangaroos for a living.'

'We move a fair bit of it, love. It's lean meat. Very low in saturated fats.' The butcher smiled. 'Want to try some?'

'I'll take a tray of the fillets. What's the best way to cook them?'

'If you put them in the fridge, take them out about twenty minutes before you want to cook them to bring the meat to room temperature, then pan-fry your fillets on high heat for four minutes each side.' The butcher wrapped her purchases in paper and placed them on the counter. 'Kangaroo tastes best if it's medium rare, so you don't want to overcook them, and it's a good idea to cover them with foil and allow the meat to rest for around ten minutes before you serve it.'

God, it's no wonder they refer to it as gourmet meat, thought Stella. As she paid for her meat, she wondered if Indigenous Australians cooked their kangaroo that way. When she thought about it, she recalled watching a documentary on the TV showing them roasting a whole kangaroo in coals and decided, probably not. She smiled as she realized only Europeans would think of kangaroo as gourmet fare.

CHAPTER 4

STELLA SETTLED in for the three-hour drive to Wirrabara, one of several small towns, villages really, situated along the western edge of the Southern Flinders Ranges, two hundred and thirty-five kilometres north of Adelaide.

'Do you have any idea of Wirrabara's place in South Australia's history, Sarge,' said Brian, as they approached the township.

'History isn't one of my strong points, Brian.'

'Well, in the early days of European settlement, they cut down the native trees covering the hills around here to provide timber for the copper mines at Moonta, Wallaroo and Burra.

'Sounds like a lot of trees,' said Stella. 'How'd they get the logs to places like Burra? That's more than a hundred kilometres from here.'

'Bullocks, I suppose. My grandfather and his father before him were bullockies. They hauled stuff all over the place, according to my grandmother.'

'So, how come you're not driving a truck, Brian?'

'Fortunately, my father's side of the family had other interests. My grandfather on that side, for instance, went into banking when he came home from the Great War, and my father followed in his footsteps,' said Brian.

'How come you ended up on the force?'

'Banking didn't seem all that attractive after my time in the army. Thought being a policeman might be a little more exciting,' said Brian.

Stella wondered if he'd made the right choice. He'd been a detective constable for nearly thirty years. She thought about the trees. 'If they cut down so many trees, how come there's still a forest here? Even after the fire, there's still millions of trees in these hills.'

'Someone in the colonial government had the foresight to establish a tree nursery up here with the intention of starting a forestry industry based on plantations. Apparently, they planted thousands of seeds from across Australia and around the world only to discover that the local conditions suit the radiata pine, which grows a lot faster than the native trees. That's why there are pine forests up here and all over the state.'

'Got any idea how big this forest is, Brian?'

'I looked that up. It's around seven thousand hectares.'

'What's that in square kilometres?'

'That would be seventy square kilometres.'

'God, what are the odds of someone finding a body in a forest that big?'

'Guess we're lucky there was a fire in the area where the body was dumped, otherwise I'd say we'd be none the wiser.'

They pulled into the local police station.

'Do you have a map of the forest, Constable?' asked Stella.

The constable pointed to a map on the wall behind her. 'It's a pretty big space, Sergeant. People occasionally get lost out there, if they're not careful. There are roads and fire tracks all through the place.'

'Do people camp in the forest?'

'There's a camping ground, Sergeant. The public aren't allowed to camp in the forest.'

'Do you need a permit to use the camping ground?'

'You can get a permit from the Forest Office, which is near the camping ground but it's self-serve if no-one's there.'

'Is the camping ground anywhere near where the skeleton was found?' said Brian.

The constable pointed to a spot on the map. 'This is where the skeleton was found. The camping ground is over here.'

'So, it's not likely anyone camping that night would have noticed anyone driving into that part of the forest,' said Stella.

'I don't think so, Sergeant, and they wouldn't have had to drive through the town either.'

'Had any luck with your local enquiries, Constable?' said Stella.

The constable shook his head. 'Five years is too long ago for most people to remember, unless it was something out of the ordinary, and seeing a car driving towards the forest, even at night, is not that unusual up here.'

'We're wondering if the killer might have had some connection to the area that would have given him local knowledge.'

'Lots of people from all over the place know about the forests here, Sergeant. You don't have to be a local.'

'I was wondering whether you'd need local knowledge to drive into the place where the bones were found and, more importantly, drive out again without getting lost.'

'I guess if he had a map or GPS he'd be able to do it.'

Stella wondered whether the killer would need a special connection to the area, beyond the casual connection of being a camper or a passing tourist, to know that it was a good place to dump a body.

Stella and Brian spent the afternoon walking from business to business in the main street with their photographs of the Semmlers, and asking people if they knew them or could remember seeing them in town. At the end of the day, they headed for the Wirrabara Hotel and checked in for the night, without having talked to anyone who could positively identify the people in their photographs.

As they sat in the dining room considering their food options, a woman approached them.

'My sister says you've been asking around about some people. You spoke to her in the craft shop. She thought I might know one of them. She thinks she looks like someone that used to live here.'

Brian took out his iPhone and found the photograph of Grant Semmler and Cassie King that he'd lifted from the case file and showed it to the woman.

'That's Cassie White. I went to school with her. She was a right nasty piece of work, always getting other kids into trouble with her lies and silly games,' said the woman.

'Why don't you sit down?' said Stella, pulling out a chair. 'What's your name?'

'Anne Walsh,' said the woman, sitting down next to Stella.

'I'm Detective Sergeant Bruno, and this is Detective Constable Rhodes. When was the last time you saw Cassie?'

'About ten years ago. She was married to a bloke that worked in the forest. Gerry King was his name. He committed suicide. She found him hanging in the shed.' Anne looked at her hands. 'Lucky they didn't have any kids. I haven't seen her since then. I heard she went south, probably to Adelaide but, to be honest, I don't really know where she went.'

'Looks like she ended up in Burra. The man she's with in that photograph is the father of the boy whose skeleton was found in the forest after the fire,' said Stella.

'Oh,' said Anne.

'Did Cassie work while she was living here?' said Stella.

'She worked for the butcher. We all thought it was funny at the time, but she did an apprenticeship with old man Henry. He was pretty upset when she left.'

'Is he still in town? I don't recall the butcher being called Henry when we visited today.'

'No, Ted Henry died a couple of years back. Heart attack, I think.'

'What was she like as an adult?' said Stella.

'She still liked to boss people around. She was a bit of a control freak, in my opinion.' Anne looked around. 'I've often wondered whether her husband killed himself to get away from her. She was very possessive.'

'Does her family still live here?' said Stella.

'No, she was an only child and her folks moved down to Adelaide not long after she and Gerry got married.'

'What about the King family?'

'Gerry's mother lives in Laura. She works at the Old Folks Home. She's one of the nurses there. I see her when I visit my grandmother.' Anne smiled. 'Gerry was from Laura. None of the boys that grew up with Cassie wanted anything to do with her. Can't say I blame them.'

'Care for a drink?' said Stella.

'No, I have to get myself into the kitchen, so I can cook whatever it is you'll be eating tonight.'

Anne stood and left them with their menus.

'Well, that's an interesting connection,' said Brian.

'Yes, and an interesting insight into the woman. Now, what are you going to have?'

On Friday morning they drove to Laura, which they had driven through on their way to Wirrabara the previous day, and called in at the Old Folks Home.

The duty nurse told them that Mrs King was rostered off on Fridays and gave them her home address, after she'd called Mrs King to see if she was available to talk with them.

Five minutes after leaving the Old Folks Home, they parked in front of her house in Samuel Street.

'Can I offer you tea or coffee?' said Mrs King.

'Black tea for me', said Brian.

'Make that two,' said Stella.

'Come and sit in the kitchen,' said Mrs King.

They sat at the kitchen table while Mrs King put the kettle on and fussed about making the tea.

'What brings you up here?'

'Are you aware of the skeleton that was found in Wirrabara Forest last week, Mrs King?'

'Saw something about that on the telly. Poor lad. I can't help thinking how his mother must be feeling,' said Mrs King, bringing the cups of tea to the table.

'We're investigating his murder,' said Stella, taking a sip of her tea.

'So why are you talking to me?'

'We'd like to know about your daughter-in-law, Cassie. She's a person of interest in our investigation.'

Mrs King put down her tea cup. 'That bitch pushed my son over the edge. He'd still be alive today if he'd listened to me. I told him she wasn't his type but he couldn't see it, could he?' She picked up her cup and sipped her tea. 'The trouble with boys, Sergeant, is they all think with their dicks when they're young, and then it's too late.'

'I'll keep that in mind. I have a fourteen-year-old.'

'Enjoy him while you can. You'll lose him if some bitch like

Cassie White ever gets her hands on him.'

'So, what precisely was she like,' said Brian.

'She was really nice when I first met her and I had to admire her pluck becoming a butcher, but once she had Gerry where she wanted him I couldn't get any sense out of him. It was like he didn't have a mind of his own. It was always Cassie says this and Cassie wants that.' She took another sip of tea.

'How long were they married,' said Stella.

'Nearly five years. He was thirty when he hung himself. She would have been twenty-eight.'

'Did he leave a note or anything?' said Stella.

'Nothing. She found him swinging when she got home from work, or at least that's the official story.'

'You doubt her account?'

'Well, there were no witnesses besides her. She could have strung him up herself for all I know. They reckon he'd been hanging there for hours. She could have killed him before she went to work.'

'What were the Coroner's findings,' said Stella.

'Death by suicide,' said Mrs King.

'Have you seen Cassie since then?'

Mrs King shook her head. 'And, I don't want to either. She packed up and left as soon as we'd buried him. You don't think she killed that lad in the forest, do you?'

'We don't know to be honest, but she's living with the boy's father.'

'I hope he's a strong sort of fellow. I wouldn't wish her on anybody.'

After interviewing Mrs King, they resumed their journey to Adelaide with Brian at the wheel.

'How do you think they got him out of the car, Brian?' said Stella, as they travelled between Clare and Watervale.

'I guess they would have known which way he'd be going to get to Spalding. It's not like there's a lot of choice.'

'See what you mean,' said Stella, looking at the map on their on-board computer.

'Good old-fashioned ambush would do the trick. All you'd have to do is block the road with your car.'

'Guess it would work even better if you had a spotlight and a rifle. You could blind him with the spotlight when he got out of the car, and he wouldn't see the rifle, would he?'

'Be all over before he realized what was going on,' said Brian.

'And, if there were two of them, one of them could have driven his car back to town after they'd picked up the body.'

'Maybe they left his car hidden behind some trees while they disposed of the body, and then came back and returned it to the pub car park to make it look like he hadn't left Clare,' said Brian.

'Why would they do that, Brian? Wouldn't that increase the risk of being seen?'

'Think about it, Sarge. If they'd left the car where they'd shot him, there would be blood on the road.'

'Be a bit risky, wouldn't it, shooting someone on a public road?'

'Not if you picked the right spot.'

'Where would that be?'

'Somewhere not near a farmhouse and with a good view in each direction.'

'It was dark, Brian.'

'Yes, and the lights of approaching cars would be visible from a long way off,' said Brian.

'I guess it wouldn't have taken all that long, especially if he'd stopped close to the other vehicle.'

Stella looked through the windscreen at the passing countryside. 'I wonder if Forensics did a thorough examination of his car or were they blindsided by the fact that it was still in the car park. You'd think there'd be some blood splatter on the car if he was shot close to his car.'

'Be in those notes, wouldn't it?'

'I wonder if they still have the car,' said Stella, flipping through the pages of her folder.

'And, there's no mention of them ever finding his car keys,' said Brian.

Stella sat in DI Williams' office after she'd briefed him on their visit to Wirrabara.

'Think we're going to need more than that, Bruno. Even if your hypothesis is correct, any good lawyer would say you were stitching up Semmler with the murder of his son. We need evidence, not supposition.'

'I can't believe no-one saw anything,' said Stella. 'There are over three thousand people living in Clare.'

'But they weren't all watching the car park of the Clare Hotel, Bruno. In fact, they were probably inside watching the Saturday night football. And, if your theory is correct, it would have been close to eleven, maybe later, when they returned the car to the car park, and who would have taken any notice. Just another car being parked.'

'The other thing that bothers me, sir, is Forensics didn't find anything out of the ordinary in his car. No blood splatter either inside or out, and nothing to connect either Semmler or King to the car. In fact, it seems all the biological material in the car was either Mark's, his girlfriend's, or his mother's.'

'His mother could just as easily have shot him, you know. She's a crack shot, and we only have her word for where she was that night after ten o'clock, when she left work. And, there are a lot less people living in Spalding to watch the streets.'

Stella cocked an eyebrow. 'What would be her motive, and how would she have managed the logistics?'

'Perhaps she had an accomplice. Maybe her new husband wanted the boy out of the way.'

Stella shook her head. 'I can't see it. I can see his motive, wanting to inflict pain on her. That's classic domestic violence, but why would she want to kill her son? It doesn't make sense.'

'The inspector leant back in his chair. 'Maybe it wasn't about the fight between the parents. What if it was something between Mark and his mother or Mark and his mother's new boyfriend?'

'There's nothing in the case notes suggesting that, sir, and it's not something I've picked up from anyone I've spoken to,' said Stella.

'Perhaps you need to speak to some more people, Bruno. When's the funeral service?'

'Monday, at ten.'

'Looks like an early start for you and Rhodes, then.'

'Do you think we should search Semmler's house and vehicles, sir?'

'What for? You're not going to find anything after five years, especially if they killed him somewhere between Clare and Spalding.'

'Car keys,' said Stella. 'He wouldn't be the first killer to have kept a souvenir from this victim. If Semmler's still got his son's car keys, we've got the connection we need.'

'I would have tossed them, if I'd killed him,' said DI Williams.

'But you didn't kill him, did you? And not everybody thinks like you, sir.'

'Guess it's worth a shot, Bruno, but do it after the funeral. If he still has them after five years, he's not likely to ditch them over the weekend.'

CHAPTER 5

AT THE END of the week, Stella caught up with Shaun for a drink after work at Georges on Waymouth.

'What have you got planned for the weekend?' said Stella, as Shaun handed her a glass of Chardonnay.

'Nothing special.'

'Want to come for dinner tomorrow night? Mum's cooking lasagna, and we could go and watch Josh play football Sunday morning,' said Stella, taking a sip of her wine.

'Lasagna. You girls know how to get a man's attention.'

'Mum noticed you enjoyed it.' Stella smiled. 'I think she might like you, and food is her weapon of choice when it comes to men.'

Shaun laughed. 'Yeah, okay, let's do that.'

'What's Sarah doing?'

'She's going out with her friends. There's some student thing on at the uni.'

Stella looked him in the eye. 'Student thing?'

Shaun shrugged his shoulders. 'You know, a concert or something like that. It's not like she gives me all the details.'

'Is there a boy involved?'

'I don't think so. She's going with a couple of her girlfriends but who knows who they're meeting up with.' Shaun sipped his wine. 'It's not like a father is the first to know these things.'

Stella thought about how things had been for her growing up. She'd shared secrets with her mother. Her poor father had always been the last to know what was going on in her life. 'I'll let you know if she tells me anything you need to worry about.'

'I know it must be difficult for her not having her mother to confide in. They were close. I always thought they were ganging up on me.'

'Oh, how did they do that?'

'They'd come to me with an issue concerning some part of Sarah's life but only to tell me how they'd decided to handle it. You know, keeping me in the loop so that I wouldn't make a fool of myself when some boy turned up to take her out.'

'I know what you mean. Mum and I did that to my father.' Stella laughed, recalling some of her father's reactions. 'Not always with the intended results, mind you. Poor Rick got an earful the first time he turned up to take me out. I was surprised he kept coming back for more.'

'Your Dad's not so bad. He's been nice to me,' said Shaun.

'You're not wet behind the ears either and, besides, he's mellowed a bit since those days.'

Shaun took another sip of wine. 'Does Josh confide in you?'

Stella thought about her son sharing his dreams with her. 'He does about most things but he spends a lot of time with his grandmother, so there isn't much I don't know about. What Mum doesn't know, Denise usually does. But boys' lives seem to be less complicated, at least at his age.'

'I guess you're right. When I was his age all I was interested in was school and sport. I didn't really get interested in girls until I was at uni,' said Shaun.

'Well, let's hope I get to be that lucky with Josh.'

'Getting any closer to working out who killed your skeleton?'

'Brian's got a theory.'

Shaun cocked his eyebrows. 'A theory?'

'Not much else to go on after five years and bugger all information from the public.'

'What's his theory?'

'He thinks it's the father.'

'What makes him think that?'

Stella counted her points off on her fingers. 'History of domestic violence between the parents, the skeleton has a head wound consistent with the calibre of rifle his father uses to shoot kangaroos, and the fact that we only have the father's new girlfriend's word for where he was that night.'

'That all sounds circumstantial to me, Stella.'

'I know. I can come up with a motive but we don't have anything connecting the father to the crime.'

'Do you want another?' said Shaun.

'Get me a mineral water. I have to drive home.'

Shaun went to the bar and bought another round of drinks.

'So, what are you intending to do?'

'We're going to search the father's place after the funeral,' said Stella.

'Why? It's five years since the boy was killed. What could you possibly hope to find there?'

'Keys. We're hoping he souvenired his son's car keys. They're the only thing we haven't found.'

'Sounds like a long shot to me.'

'It probably is but we need to cover that possibility.'

Brian drove into the yard next to the small stone church of St Augustine and parked among the cars in the field of grass.

'Looks like a good-sized crowd,' said Stella.

'Well, he was a popular lad after all,' said Brian, 'if we can believe what we've heard about him.'

The small church was almost filled to capacity when they entered and they were lucky to get seats in a rear pew. Stella noted the mourners sitting in front of them were mostly young men, and assumed they were the boys Mark had played football with. She spotted Dave Ross and his family sitting in the pew behind Pam and Peter Ross.

As the coffin was wheeled to the front of the church, she saw that Grant Semmler and Cassie King were in the front pew opposite Pam and Peter Ross with another couple that looked like Grant's brother and his wife. From behind, Grant did not look comfortable in his dark suit and Stella wondered how many times he'd worn a suit in his life.

The mourners seated on the side behind Pam were mostly older people, and Stella assumed they were friends of the family and townspeople who had come to support Pam and Grant in their moment of shared sadness.

It was a subdued service. There was no eulogy and no Power-Point presentation of photographs from Mark's life. The words of consolation offered by the priest were generic and betrayed the fact he hadn't known Mark during his short life.

After the service, they travelled out to the cemetery in the convoy of cars carrying mourners and watched as the priest said the final prayers, and the coffin was lowered into the grave.

Stella noticed Grant Semmler, who had stood apart from Pam Ross until the coffin had started to descend into the grave, walk over to Pam and say something to her before heading to his car and driving away with Cassie King.

The mourners gathered in the Spalding Community Centre to share a lunch provided by the Country Women's Association and to talk about Mark Semmler and the mystery of his untimely death.

Stella and Brian mingled with the crowd, listening to the conversations going on around them and answering questions from people interested in the progress of their investigation.

As they were about to leave, the man Stella thought was Grant Semmler's brother approached them.

'Pam tells me you're the police investigating my nephew's death,' he said.

'Yes. I'm Detective Sergeant Bruno and this is Detective Constable Rhodes.'

The man shook Stella's hand. 'It must be a hard job finding any clues after five years. Are you making any progress?'

Stella shook her head. 'It seems no-one saw anything or, at least, no-one's come forward with any information that could help us.'

'What are you doing here?'

'Sometimes funerals prompt memories when people are dwelling on the past,' said Stella.

'You know, Sergeant, I don't live all that far from Grant's place. You can't see his house from my place but, you know, at night sound travels and I often hear his truck coming and going when he goes shooting.' He scratched his head. 'I often think about the night Mark disappeared. I've tried to recollect what I heard and connect it with what Grant told me he'd done that night.'

Stella could see pain in his eyes and wondered what he was going to tell her.

'I don't think they came home after the football that night. I didn't hear them leave to go shooting and that could be because I was inside the house, but I'm a light sleeper, Sergeant, and I heard them come home sometime after midnight, in two cars.' He stopped and looked at Stella. 'They only ever take his truck when they go shooting.'

'What are you trying to tell me, Mr Semmler?' said Stella.

'I don't think you can trust my brother, Sergeant. He did some horrible things to Pam that I've never forgiven him for, and I'm worried he might have killed Mark to hurt her. At the very least, I don't think he's told you the truth about where he was that night.'

'Are you willing to make a formal statement, Mr Semmler?'

Mr Semmler looked at his hands. 'Yes.'

Grant stood outside the church. He hadn't been inside St Augustine's since the day he'd married Pam. He hadn't been inside any church since Pam had left him. She was the one that believed in God and had dragged him along to services when they'd been a married couple. These days he believed in nothing and preferred it that way.

He felt constrained in his suit, which he hadn't worn for years. He'd only worn it because Cassie had insisted and fussed over how respectable it made him look. If he'd had his way, he would have worn his work clothes. He knew he would have been comfortable in his work clothes even if he'd looked less respectable. He looked at Cassie in her black dress and realized she'd look good in anything she chose to wear. But, it wasn't her outward appearance that concerned him. Somehow, she'd taken control of his soul. If he hadn't listened to her he wouldn't be standing outside St Augustine's dreading to go inside and face the consequences of his moment of weakness.

He wasn't prepared for the crowd inside the church. He'd thought it would be a small, quiet affair. He hadn't known how popular Mark had been with his friends. Seeing them all in the church only added to the pain of knowing that he hadn't really known the boy, and had only seen him as something Pam loved. He was relieved when his brother and his wife joined them. They at least were familiar.

He looked at the people sitting in the pews behind Pam and Peter Ross. He could see they had plenty of friends. He stole a look across the church at Pam. With her new man beside her, she seemed calm and at peace with what was going on.

It wasn't supposed to work out like this. He was the one that was supposed to feel good. She was the one that was supposed to be devastated by the loss of her darling boy.

He listened as the priest droned on. He couldn't wait for the service to be over. As he walked out of the church in the family group behind the coffin, he spotted the policewoman that was investigating Mark's death and wondered what she was doing at the funeral.

At the graveside, he felt hollow. He watched as Pam stood strong and dropped a rose onto Mark's coffin. Then it was his turn.

When he'd dropped the flower, he turned to Pam.

'I'm sorry, Pam. I'm sorry it turned out like this.'

Then, without waiting for her response, he turned and walked to the car, with Cassie running to catch up with him.

'Where are you going?' said Cassie, as she reached him.

'Home!'

Grant was relieved she had the sense not to argue and it dawned on him she probably wasn't feeling all that comfortable being there either.

They drove back to Burra in silence.

As soon as they got home, he changed out of his suit into his work clothes and sat out on the veranda with the dog.

'Do you want a beer?' said Cassie from the kitchen.

'Thanks.'

She came out with a can of beer in each hand. 'Do you want to talk?'

He pulled the ring on the can, raised the beer to his lips and took a long drink. Then he placed the can on the table between them.

'I'm going into town to turn myself in.'

'What did you say?'

'I'm turning myself in. I never should have listened to you.'

'But why? The police have no idea what happened.'

'I don't really give a shit about the police. I'm the one that has to live with what I did.' He looked at her. 'And, I can't do it anymore.'

Grant stood.

'But what about me?'

Grant turned and looked at her. 'What about you?'

He stepped off the veranda and started walking across the yard to the shed.

CHAPTER 6

Stella wasn't expecting to see a dead dog in the yard between the house and the shed when they reached the end of Grant Semmler's tree-lined driveway.

'Something's not right here, Sarge,' said Brian, bringing the car to a stop at the edge of the yard.

Stella looked across the yard to the shed. 'There are only two vehicles in the shed. Her Mazda's not there.'

Brian got out of the car and walked over to the dead dog. 'Shit! This dog's been shot in the head.' He turned slowly and surveyed the yard and then the interior of the shed. 'There's someone on the ground between those cars.'

Stella waited near the car while Brian walked over to the shed and checked the person on the ground.

'It's Semmler. He's dead!'

Brian walked back to where Stella was standing. 'He's been shot through the head, same as the dog.'

'We'd better take a look in the house,' said Stella.

They walked over to the house and stepped up onto the veranda, where two beer cans sat on the table. 'Anybody there?' said Stella, standing outside the back door.

'Go and get the plastic shoes and some gloves,' said Stella. 'I'll wait here.'

When they'd covered their shoes and slipped on their gloves, Stella tested the back door. It wasn't locked. 'Let's have a look inside.'

They looked in each room. There was nobody in the house but there was a rifle with telescopic sights on the kitchen table.

'Looks like one of his roo shooting rifles,' said Brian. 'It's a Howa.'

'I wonder what happened here?' said Stella, taking out her mobile phone. 'I hope we've got coverage out here.' She looked at the bars on her phone and then called Operations and explained their situation.

'Be a couple of hours before Forensics get here,' said Stella. 'Guess we'd better make ourselves comfortable.'

Brian shifted the car into the shade at the end of the driveway and they sat to wait for Forensics.

Stella called DI Williams and briefed him on what they'd found.

'Better get an APB out on Cassie King as soon as you have all the details, Bruno.'

Stella pulled out her case folder, collated the details she needed for an APB and then placed a call to Operations to put it into effect.

'I wonder where she's gone,' said Brian.

'Where would you go, Brian, if you were in her shoes?'

'I'd head bush.'

'She'd have taken the Toyota if she was going bush, I reckon. My guess is she's gone to Adelaide to disappear or maybe interstate.'

'If she shot him yesterday, she could be interstate already,' said Brian. 'If she's got a passport, she could even be out of the country by now.'

'What if she's not the shooter? What if she's been taken hostage?' said Stella.

'How likely do you think that is, Sarge?'

'Not likely, to be honest, but I guess we won't know until we get a chance to search the place properly.'

Forensics' crime scene investigators arrived at twelve thirty-six. Stella explained to them what she and Brian had done and where they'd been within the crime scene.

After examining Grant Semmler's body, Dr Steve Wright gave Stella an estimated time of death as sometime in the previous twenty-four hours.

'I know he was alive at eleven forty-five yesterday morning, Steve. That's when he left the funeral, so maybe she shot him not long after they got home,' said Stella, 'assuming she's the shooter.'

'So, she could have several hours head start on you,' said Steve. ' I guess she wouldn't have hung about after she'd done the deed.'

'I've got an APB out on her. We'll find her.'

'What were you doing here, anyway, Stella?'

'We'd come to search the place, to see if we could find his son's car keys,' said Stella.

'That's a bit of a long shot after five years, isn't it?'

'Thought it was the best shot available to me at the time,' said Stella. 'I'm hoping he souvenired them.'

'How will you recognize them if you find them?' said Steve.

'His mother told us five years ago that he had a keyring with the BSR Tigers' logo and that the disc with the logo has the number eighteen stamped on the back.'

'Why don't you start your search here in the shed while the boys are working on the house?'

Stella pulled her gloves back on and looked through the interior of the Valiant while Brian checked the Toyota.

'Over here, Sarge. They were at the back of the glovebox.' Brian held up a bunch of keys with a black disc embossed with the face of a golden tiger and the words BSR Tigers. 'The numerals one eight are stamped on the back.'

'Bag it, Brian.'

'Looks more like they might have been forgotten than souvenired,' said Brian.

'Either way, Brian, they're here, and that's the connection we were looking for.'

One of the crime scene investigators approached Stella.

'Sergeant Bruno, there are some clear prints on that rifle in the kitchen. Look's like it's only been handled by two people, and one of them is the deceased. The other set matches some of the prints in the kitchen and the bathroom.'

'I'd be willing to bet the other lot belong to Cassie King,' said Stella.

'Do we know how many guns this bloke has?'

'Two last time I looked at the register,' said Brian. 'Both Howas.'

'Well, they're both here, then. The other one is still in the gun cupboard.'

'That's a relief,' said Stella.

'Let's not forget she's a trained butcher, Sarge,' said Brian. 'She could still be dangerous if she's got a knife on her.'

'I wonder why she shot him,' said Stella. 'Bit drastic for a lovers' tiff, don't you think?'

'He didn't look too happy to me yesterday, Sarge. Perhaps the funeral was just too much for him. Perhaps remorse got to him and they argued over what he wanted to do about it.'

'She would have had to have been in on it, Brian. It had to have been a two-person operation to get his car back into Clare,' said Stella, 'and, she's the most likely candidate for being his accomplice.'

They followed the crime scene investigator into the house and searched through the desk in the second bedroom that Grant had used as his office, looking for bank statements and mobile phone accounts and not finding any.

'Guess he must have been doing his banking and bill paying online,' said Brian.

'There's no computer in here,' said Stella.

'But there's a modem with a wireless router connected to the phone line in the front room,' said Brian. 'I remember seeing it the day we interviewed them.'

'But is there any sign he actually had a computer in here?' said Stella.

Brian looked closely at the desktop and then stood back and looked at it again from near the window. 'There's been a laptop on this desk. Look at that patch not covered in dust.' He pointed to a dark covered rectangle on the desktop in front of the chair.

'She must have taken his computer with her,' said Stella.

'Let's just check with the CSI boys to see if they found a computer anywhere else in the house,' said Brian.

When they learnt that the crime scene investigators had not seen a computer, Stella checked the bathroom and the wardrobe in the main bedroom.

'I'd say she shot him, Brian,' said Stella, closing the door to the wardrobe. 'She'd hardly have taken her clothes and toiletries if she'd been taken hostage by someone else. Besides, why would someone only shoot him and not her?'

As they walked across the yard to their car to drive back to Adelaide, the Coroner's van arrived to collect the body.

'Let's get out of here, Brian. I don't fancy following them back to town.'

Although Stella suspected Cassie King had fled into the city to hide among the million or so people that lived in the Adelaide metropolitan area, she knew it was a little more difficult to hide than most people thought.

While Brian attempted to trace Cassie using the mobile phone number they had on file for her, Stella worked her way through the banks to find out which of them serviced Grant Semmler and Cassie King. It was slow work.

Eventually, she discovered that Grant had an account with Bank SA and, when she asked the question, the bank's liaison officer told her that most of the money in his account, a little over five thousand dollars, had been transferred to an account in the name of C. King at People's Choice Credit Union, shortly after two o'clock on Monday afternoon.

When she spoke to the liaison officer at People's Choice Credit Union, she learnt that Cassie had a Visa debit card attached to her account, and had withdrawn a thousand dollars in cash from an ATM on Norwood Parade shortly after eight pm on Monday night, but had not used the card since. Stella requested that Cassie's account be monitored and that she be informed as soon as the card was used again.

'Any luck, Brian?'

'They reckon she's turned her phone off. The last known location is Burra on Monday at three in the afternoon.'

'Shit! She's a little smarter than I thought. She's withdrawn cash from an ATM in Norwood, a thousand dollars. She could be anywhere by now.'

'Guess our best hope is she hasn't ditched the car,' said Brian.

'A thousand dollars won't go far, especially if she's staying in a motel. She'll have to use her card again at some point.'

'What if she's got friends?'

Stella shrugged her shoulders. 'We'll just have to hope they have a conscience when they see the news story that's going out tonight.'

'Who's fronting that?'

Stella looked at her watch. 'I'd better go and touch up my face. I need to be in the media room with DI Williams in fifteen minutes.'

Stella thought DI Williams looked dapper in his dark grey suit, white shirt and red tie. He relished being in front of the cameras, which suited her fine. She preferred to stand in the background and let him handle the questions.

The spotlights came on and DI Williams stepped up to the microphone. Behind him, a five-year-old image of Cassie King from the original missing persons file filled the wall.

She listened as he explained who Cassie was and why they were asking for the public's help to find her.

'Is she dangerous?' a voice called from the throng.

'She knows how to use a knife and although she shot her partner, we don't think she's armed. All the same, people should ring the Crime Stoppers hotline and not approach her,' said DI Williams.

'Do you have any idea where she might be?' asked another reporter.

'The last known location we have for her is the RediATM on Norwood parade at approximately eight pm on Monday night,' said DI Williams. 'We would appreciate any information anyone has about her movements after that time.'

After the press conference, Stella returned to the squad room and checked her inbox for any messages from People's Choice. Nothing.

'This is the part I hate,' said Brian. 'The waiting to see if anybody calls.'

'Know what you mean.'

'When are they doing the autopsy?' said Brian.

'Tomorrow morning. It's at nine-thirty. Do you want to go?'

'Okay, I'll do it. Guess he's not going to tell us much we don't already know.'

Cassie sat in the cabin she'd rented at the Levi Park Caravan Park and watched the news on the TV mounted on the wall. There was a segment on the shooting at Burra and an appeal from the police for help in locating the suspected killer, Cassie King.

'You're going to have to do better than that,' she laughed, when she saw the images they were using. The image of the car was a stock image with her registration number under it and the photograph of her was at least five years old and showed her with shoulder length blonde hair.

Most of that hair was now in the bin in the bathroom of the cabin, and the short hair on her head was jet black, thanks to the hair dye she'd washed through it. She'd even worn it up and under a cap when she'd booked into the caravan park for the week under the name of Cassandra White, the name on her driver's licence.

She looked out at her car parked next to the cabin and wondered how long it would take the police to work out she'd switched the plates with those on Grant's Valiant. Maybe they'd never wake up to that one but she wondered what she was going to do for money if they froze her account, and if the police did such things.

She switched off the TV and cursed Grant for being such a gutless wonder. They'd gotten away with it for five years. He'd been keen when she'd first suggested killing Mark to punish Pam. He'd been easy to manipulate with sex back then. She shrugged her shoulders and wondered what had happened to make him lose his nerve. Surely, he hadn't felt sorry for that stupid bitch that had hurt him so badly.

Maybe it hadn't been such a good idea going to the funeral, she thought, but she didn't think they'd had much choice about going in any case.

She couldn't believe that Grant had decided to turn himself in after the funeral without a second thought as to what that would mean for her. Obviously, she didn't mean anything to him.

She wondered if she'd acted in haste when she'd grabbed his rifle and shot him. Pity about the dog, though. Stupid animal should have left her alone.

Too late now though, she thought. She'd killed him. Now they wanted her for two murders but there was no way they were going to catch her. She had her plan worked out and, in the morning, she'd be gone. She'd be someone else.

She waited until it was dark, then drove over to the ATM on Norwood Parade and withdrew another thousand dollars, and cursed them for imposing a daily limit on the amount of cash she could withdraw.

CHAPTER 7

BRIAN LOOKED through the crime scene photographs while he was waiting to go downstairs to Grant Semmler's autopsy. They'd taken a shot of the body on the ground between the Valiant and the Toyota from outside the shed that captured the number plates on both vehicles.

Something's not right here, thought Brian. I don't remember the registration number on that Valiant starting with an S. He logged onto the Motor Vehicle Registration database and keyed in the registration number showing on the Valiant.

The database display informed him that the number was assigned to a Mazda 323 owned by a Cassandra King living in Burra. He noticed there was no driver's licence number in that field and double checked. It looked like Cassandra King didn't have a driver's licence. He checked his notes for her maiden name and tried a query under Cassandra White. 'Bingo!' said Brian.

He keyed in Grant Semmler with a location of Burra. The display listed two vehicles. A Toyota with a registration number that matched the one in the crime scene photograph, and a Chrysler Valiant with a registration number of RKX-321.

'Shit! She's switched the plates.'

'What are you talking about, Brian?'

'Here, look at this.'

Stella walked over to his desk.

'See, that?' Brian pointed at the photograph on his desk. 'That's the number plate from her Mazda.'

'You think she's put the plates from the Valiant onto her car?' said Stella.

'Would explain why no-one's seen it, wouldn't it? And, Sarge, her driver's licence is in the name of White. She could be using that as ID to book in if she's paying cash.'

'Good work, Brian.' Stella looked at her watch. 'You'd better get a move on or you'll be late for the autopsy. I'll get on to Operations and update our search criteria.'

Two hours after she'd released the update, Stella received a call through the Crime Stoppers hotline.

'Detective Sergeant Bruno. You wanted to talk to me?'

'I think we had that woman you're looking for staying here.'

'Where are you?'

'At the Levi Park Caravan Park. I'm the manager.'

'Okay, what makes you think she was staying there?'

'We had a woman book into one of the cabins on Monday night. She paid cash, so I asked for ID. She gave me a driver's licence in the name of Cassandra White, and I recorded the registration number of her car. It was RKX-321.'

'Is she still there?'

'She booked for a week but the cleaner reckons she's gone. All of her stuff is gone from the cabin.'

'Okay. Did anyone see her leave?'

'She drove out at eight fifteen this morning, according to the computer. She's still got the key to her cabin. Oh, and something else you might want to know. The cleaner says she found a bag of blonde hair and a black hair dye box in the bin. I think she may have changed her appearance.'

'I'll send someone out to check over that cabin and collect that bag of rubbish and, sir, thank you for calling.'

'Always glad to help, Sergeant.'

Stella felt elated. The call was the first real breakthrough they'd had since asking the public for help. She called Operations and asked them to alert patrols that their suspect had been at the Levi Park Caravan Park and was on the move.

After speaking with Operations, she called DI Williams and updated him on their progress.

Stella looked at the screen of her computer and wondered if Cassie was monitoring the news and whether she'd be aware they'd discovered she'd switched number plates. If she was still in the metropolitan area, Stella guessed she'd ditch the car if she realized it had become a liability. But, thought Stella, if Cassie had headed out of town she wouldn't have that luxury, especially if she was travelling towards the border across the great Australian emptiness.

Brian stood to one side of the stainless steel bench as Dr Wright conducted the post mortem examination of Grant Semmler's body. He always felt he shouldn't be present when someone's body was being asked to yield its secrets. It always seemed like an intrusion to Brian, and he hoped nobody would have to watch them open up his body and poke around inside it looking for the reason he was dead.

He'd been to enough autopsies since becoming a detective that they'd lost their magic and had become somewhat routine. He hardly noticed the smell any more, unless it was a bad one. At least Grant Semmler's body hadn't been out in the open for weeks or months before being found. That was something to give thanks for, thought Brian. He didn't particularly enjoy the autopsies of badly decayed bodies.

Apart from the wound to the head, Brian thought the body looked in good shape at the start of the procedure.

It was a different story running through his head by the time Dr Wright had finished removing all the major organs and examining them in fine detail. Brian always wondered why they went to the trouble of examining every part of the body when it was perfectly clear to everybody in the room how the deceased had been killed.

'So, what do I tell the boss?' said Brian, as Dr Wright wrapped up the post mortem.

'Death by gunshot wound to the head, consistent with a round fired from the weapon found at the crime scene. And, Brian, tell DS Bruno that the wound is similar to the one in young Semmler's skull.'

'We thought it might be, Doc.'

***

Sergeant Malcolm Russell had been stationed in Pinnaroo, the last town on the South Australian side of the border for travellers heading to Victoria along the Mallee Highway, for two years.

Not much had happened in that time to disturb Sergeant Russell and his constable, apart from the occasional speeding motorist in a hurry to get somewhere. They started most days reading the Advertiser at their desks in the police station, waiting for something to happen before deciding to go out and monitor the traffic on the highway with their speed camera or to spend the day talking to the locals as they did their rounds.

Sergeant Russell had just topped up his coffee when the telephone on his desk rang.

'Got some excitement for you, Mal,' said the dispatcher from Operations.

'Oh, what's up?'

'That woman everyone's been looking for down here is heading your way. She should be arriving in the next twenty minutes or so. We've just had a call from a guy driving a TNT truck outside Lameroo that he's following a blue Mazda 323 with registration number RKX-321, and it's coming to you.'

'Okay, we're on it.'

Sergeant Russell turned to his constable.

'Jake, we need to set up a road block to intercept cars coming in from Lameroo. The woman they reckon shot that bloke in Burra is headed our way. It's a blue Mazda 323, rego RKX-321, and there's a TNT truck behind her.'

'Is she armed?'

'No-one knows, Jake, so be careful.'

'How we gonna do this, Sarge?' said Jake.

'Let's block the road at the sixty K sign. We only have to worry about the traffic coming from Lameroo. There shouldn't be much at this time of the day.'

'See you there, Sarge.'

Five minutes later, they parked their vehicles across the road where the speed limit changed from eighty to sixty kilometres per hour on the edge of town, leaving enough room for them to wave through any cars heading towards Lameroo, and waited.

When he spotted the TNT truck approaching, Sergeant Russell moved his vehicle to block the roadway, then stood on the road and indicated to the driver of the blue Mazda in front of the slowing TNT truck to pull over and stop.

When the Mazda came to a stop, the driver of the TNT truck

pulled up behind the Mazda and boxed it in between his truck and the patrol car and police Land Cruiser.

Sergeant Russell whipped his pistol from his holster, pointed it at the woman behind the wheel of the Mazda, and opened the driver's side door of the car.

'Out of the car!'

'What's going on?'

'Get out of the car and place your hands on your head!'

The woman slowly extricated herself from the car and complied with his order.

'Where's your driver's licence?'

'In my handbag. I'll get it for you.'

'Stay where you are! Jake, get her handbag!'

Jake opened the passenger side door of the Mazda, located her handbag on the back seat of the car and searched through it until he found her driver's licence in a purse. 'Cassandra White,' said Jake, reading the name on the driver's licence.

'Hands behind your back!'

Cassie complied. Sergeant Russell handcuffed her, told her she was under arrest for the murder of Grant Semmler and informed her of her rights. Then, he placed her in the secure section at the back of the Land Cruiser. When he'd locked her in, he walked over to the driver of the TNT truck and extended his hand.

'You okay, mate?'

The driver shook hands with him. 'Yeah. You boys don't muck around, do you?"

Sergeant Russell smiled. 'How'd you know it was her?'

'She passed me on the way out of Lameroo, right on the ten o'clock news. I couldn't believe it. They read out the rego of the car right in front of me, so I called it in on the CB.'

'Thanks. We wouldn't have caught her without your help.'

CHAPTER 8

STELLA WAS RELIEVED when DI Williams announced he'd watch their confrontation of Cassie King from the observation room behind the two-way glass in the interview room. The inspector's decision told her that he trusted that she and Brian would get the results they deserved.

Stella almost didn't recognize the woman in the interview room as Cassie King. She hadn't been expecting the short spiky head of jet-black hair that made Cassie look like something out of a punk rock magazine.

Brian started the interview by explaining the process to Cassie and reminding her of her rights.

Cassie looked at the duty lawyer sitting next to her and stated her name when Brian asked her to say it to record who was present at the interview.

'Ms King, you understand we've arrested you for the murder of Grant Semmler, don't you?' said Stella.

'I didn't even know he was dead, so how could I have murdered him?'

'So, what's the reason for your drastic change in hairstyle, Ms King?'

'Time for a change.' Cassie turned her head back and forth showing off her new haircut. 'Do you like it?'

Stella took a photograph out of her folder and placed it on the table in front of Cassie.

'This was taken at Burra on Tuesday afternoon. That's Grant's body between the vehicles in the shed.'

Cassie looked at the photograph and then at Stella. 'He's dead?'

'I think you already know that, Ms King.' Stella pointed at the number plate on the Valiant. 'That's Grant's car but that's the number plate from your Mazda. Mind telling me why you switched number plates, Ms King?'

Cassie said nothing in response to Stella's question.

Stella placed a photograph of a blue Mazda 323 on the table. 'This is the car you were driving when you were arrested.' Stella tapped the number plate on the car with her fingernail. 'That's the registration number assigned to Grant's Valiant. You do realize that's an offence under the Traffic Act, don't you?'

'So, charge me! It doesn't mean I had anything to do with Grant's murder.'

Cassie folded her arms.

Stella placed a photograph of a rifle resting on a white table-cloth on the table in front of Cassie.

'This is a photograph of the rifle found on the kitchen table in the house you shared with Grant Semmler.'

'Looks like one of his roo shooting rifles. He had two of them,' said Cassie.

'We've tested this one, Ms King. The bullet that killed Grant was fired from this rifle.'

'Well, that's fucking poetic, isn't it? I suppose the next thing you're going to tell me is he was shot through the head,' said Cassie.

'Why would you think that?'

'He spent his entire working life shooting kangaroos through the head. You should have seen the hate mail he got from bloody animal rights activists.' Cassie looked Stella in the eye. 'Wouldn't surprise me if one of them finally carried out their threat. They were always saying they'd shoot him through the head like he did to kangaroos.'

Stella took a deep breath and counted to five. She hadn't expected that line of argument. She took another deep breath and reminded herself that she was dealing with someone who'd had time to think about her answers.

'There are only two sets of prints on this rifle, Ms King. Grant's and yours.'

'That's not surprising. We both used it to shoot kangaroos.'

'Are you suggesting someone else used this rifle to kill Grant?'

'Well, it wasn't me. They must have been wearing gloves or something if they didn't leave any fingerprints.'

'If that was the case, Ms King, we wouldn't have been able to lift a clear print of your finger from the trigger. Any existing prints on the trigger would have been damaged by anybody wearing gloves pulling the trigger,' said Stella.

Cassie said nothing.

'Were you surprised that we found his body so quickly?' said Stella.

Cassie didn't take the bait.

'Do you know why we were at Grant's the day after Mark's funeral?'

Cassie shook her head.

'Can you answer that question for the recording, please?' said Brian.

'No. Why would I?' said Cassie.

'Did you have much to do with Grant's brother?' said Stella.

'Not much. They didn't get on. Something to do with Pam, I think.'

'At Mark's funeral, he told me about something that had been bothering him since we'd worked out Mark had been shot.'

'Oh, what was that?' said Cassie.

'He told me that on the night Mark disappeared, he heard you and Grant coming home after midnight.'

'Yeah, that would be right. We went shooting after the football.'

'I understand you took the Toyota out when you went roo shooting. I mean, after all, it's been especially set up for that purpose, hasn't it?'

'Yeah. Of course, we took the Toyota. You'd hardly want to take an ordinary car out where we went shooting. There aren't any roads out there.'

'What he told me was he remembered the sound of two cars driving up your driveway that night, not one.'

'He must have been dreaming.'

'And, then there's this.' Stella took the plastic evidence bag out of her folder and held it up for Cassie to see. 'This is Mark's keyring. We found it in the glovebox of the Toyota.'

'Fuck! I told him to get rid of that.' Cassie covered her mouth with her hand.

Stella knew she had her right where she wanted her.

'Perhaps you might want to tell us how he came to have it.'

Cassie collapsed back into her chair and held her head in her hands.

Stella waited, and imagined DI Williams wetting his pants with excitement behind the glass separating them. She knew the story would flow once Cassie started talking.

'Grant was a broken man when I met him. That stupid bitch had ruined his life. She'd turned his own son against him. Can you imagine that?' Cassie paused, and then continued. 'He was so screwed up it took him ages to see I was right about what to do with Mark, and it drove the silly bitch nuts not knowing what had happened to him.' Cassie looked at Stella. 'Yeah, it was my idea. I had to explain it to him. Men are so thick sometimes. It was only when he finally got it that he started reaching out to Mark, to gain his confidence.' She laughed. 'And, we got away with it. No-one had any idea we'd done it, and Pam was devastated. That was the best bit.' Cassie leant back in her chair. 'If it hadn't been for that bloody fire no-one would ever have found out.'

'How did you do it?' said Stella.

'Did what those bloody coppers did to me at Pinnaroo. Blocked the road with our cars. Grant shot him when he got out of his car. It was too easy.'

'Who drove his car back to Clare?' said Stella.

'Grant did that after we'd dumped the body in the forest. I followed him and drove him back to the Toyota. That's when I told him to get rid of Mark's bloody keys.'

'So, why did you shoot Grant?'

'The bastard wanted to turn himself in. After all I'd done for him, he didn't give a shit about what happened to me.'

DI Williams was waiting for them when they exited the interview room. Stella thought he looked like the proud father of a child that had just kicked the winning goal in the grand final.

'Good work, Bruno!'

'It was Brian's theory, sir. He thought Mark had been shot by his father right from the start.'

'Well, you've nailed her between you. Well done.'

They walked down the corridor towards the lift lobby.

'Might be a good idea to meet with Mrs Ross, Bruno. I think we owe her at least that much before this goes public.'

Stella looked at her watch. 'We'll just have a bite to eat and head up to Spalding, sir.'

'Let me know when you've spoken to her, Bruno.'

Stella and Brian dumped their notes in the squad room and then took the lift down to the ground and headed for the coffee shop for lunch.

***

Pam Ross was waiting for them at home and led them into the living room where they'd interviewed her after identifying the skeleton found in Wirrabara Forest as being her son's.

Stella waited until Pam had served them tea and cake.

'As I mentioned on the phone, Mrs Ross, there have been some developments we need to share with you before they become public knowledge,' said Stella.

'Is this about Mark or Grant?' said Pam.

'Both, actually.'

Stella took a sip of her tea and replaced the cup in its saucer. 'We've arrested Cassie for Grant's murder, and she's made certain statements about Mark's death.'

'Oh.'

'We found Mark's keyring in the glovebox of Grant's Toyota, the one he used for shooting.'

Pam's eyes opened wide. 'How did they end up there?' She put down her cup.

'According to Cassie, Grant drove Mark's car back to Clare after they shot him and disposed of his body in the forest at Wirrabara.'

Pam looked from Stella to Brian. 'Why would Grant shoot Mark? I don't understand. He was going out of his way to re-establish a relationship with him.'

'Cassie persuaded him it would be the best way to pay you back for what you'd done to him.'

'What I'd done to him! That's a bit rich. He's the one that destroyed our marriage by bashing me up.'

Stella waited while Pam composed herself.

'Yes, I understand that, but that's obviously not how he saw it, which is fairly common for men who abuse their wives.' Stella looked at Pam. 'They generally don't accept responsibility for their actions and they always blame the wife. I'm sure you're aware of that part.'

Pam leant back in her chair.

'You're not wrong there, Sergeant. As far as Grant was concerned, it was always my fault, even when it wasn't. That's why I left him in the end. I couldn't get him to see reason and I couldn't get him to stop hitting me.' Pam looked up and smiled. 'Wish I'd met Peter first. He's wonderful and he's never abused me like Grant did.'

'I'm happy to hear that, Mrs Ross.'

'What happens now?' said Pam.

'This will be on the news tonight, Mrs Ross. It might be a while before the media frenzy dies down.'

Josh had gone to bed at ten and left Stella and Shaun on the couch in front of the television. At eleven, when the film they'd been watching finished, Stella turned off the TV.

'Want a refill?'

Shaun held out his glass.

Stella took their glasses into the kitchen and refilled them with cold white wine from the bottle in the refrigerator.

'What time do we have to get up in the morning?' said Shaun, when she handed him his glass.

'His game's at ten.'

Shaun yawned and stretched across the couch, taking care not to spill his wine. 'Is he going with Stefano?'

'He'll be gone before you're awake.' Stella laughed. 'They have to be there at nine.'

Shaun made room for her to sit next to him on the couch. 'So, you must be feeling proud of yourself? Another killer off the streets.'

Stella snuggled up to him on the couch. 'Brian's win this time. I just went along for the ride. He was the one that joined all the dots.'

'If he's so clever, how come he's still only a detective constable?'

'That's a question you'll have to ask him, but I think he likes things the way they are.'

Shaun drank some of his wine.

'Still can't get my head around that bloke shooting his own son. I could never hurt Sarah or Josh, and he's not even my child.'

'People do all sorts of irrational things, sweetheart, for reasons we'll never understand. He was beating up his wife before she left him, and that's something I've never understood.'

'Me neither,' said Shaun, letting his hand slide down her shoulder and onto her breast.

'Do you want to go to bed?'

'Hmm. That sounds like an invitation I shouldn't refuse.'

If you enjoyed **The Identity Thief Collection,** you can help other readers share your enjoyment by telling them about the book and writing a review.

Drop by at **www.petermulraney.com** and join my **Crime Readers Group** to download a free copy of **Deadly Sands** and be one of the first to know when my next book will be released.

Living Alone (Collection)

Living Alone Journal

Everyday Business Skills

Everyday Project Management

Everyday Productivity

Everyday Money Management

Writings of the Mystic

Sharing the Journey: Reflections of a Reluctant Mystic

A Question of Perspective

My Life is My Responsibility: Insights for Conscious Living

I Am Affirmations: The Power of Words

Beyond the Words: Reflections on I Am Affirmations

Mystical Journey: A Handbook for Modern Mystics

Sharing the Journey Coloring Books

Mandalas

Mandalas by 3

Sharing the Journey Coloring Journals

Sharing the Journey Coloring Journal

Discovery

Reflection